# LOST
# HILLS

Center Point
Large Print

**This Large Print Book carries the
Seal of Approval of N.A.V.H.**

# LOST HILLS

## LEE GOLDBERG

CENTER POINT LARGE PRINT
THORNDIKE, MAINE

This Center Point Large Print edition
is published in the year 2020 by arrangement with
Amazon Publishing, www.apub.com.

The text of this Large Print edition is unabridged.
In other aspects, this book may vary
from the original edition.
Printed in the United States of America
on permanent paper.
Set in 16-point Times New Roman type.

ISBN: 978-1-64358-622-9

The Library of Congress has cataloged this record
under Library of Congress Control Number: 2020932626

*For Valerie and Maddie*

# LOST
# HILLS

# CHAPTER ONE

The northern stretch of Mulholland Highway ended in a T intersection with Mulholland Drive. It was an intersection that generated lots of confusion, and not only because of the nearly identical street names. It was also the intersection of two cities, three neighborhoods, two law enforcement jurisdictions, and on this hot, smoggy Thursday afternoon in December, life and death.

Los Angeles County Sheriff's Department homicide detectives Eve Ronin and Duncan Pavone headed to that intersection. They were driving east on Mulholland Drive in a plain-wrap Ford Explorer to investigate a possible homicide called in by the LAPD.

"There's only one reason the LAPD would call us on a corpse," Duncan said, sitting in the passenger seat and wiping donut crumbs from his big belly, which he used like an airplane tray table. "To tell us that it's on our side of the line and not theirs."

Jurisdictional disputes were inevitable, given the geography. The sheriff's department was responsible for law enforcement in Malibu, the Santa Monica Mountains, and the surrounding communities of Westlake Village, Agoura Hills,

9

Hidden Hills, and Calabasas. It was an enforcement area bordered by Ventura County to the west and northwest, the City of Los Angeles to the east and northeast, and Santa Monica Bay to the south. The intersection of Mulholland and Mulholland, on the northern lowlands of the Santa Monica Mountains, was the boundary between the Woodland Hills section of Los Angeles and the City of Calabasas.

Eve had only been in the Robbery-Homicide Division, and working out of the Lost Hills station in Calabasas, for three months and this was her first encounter with a jurisdictional dispute. She was keenly aware of what she didn't know and so was everybody else around her.

"How do you resolve the situation if it isn't clear-cut?" Eve asked, even though she knew the question would reinforce the low opinion that Duncan and the other detectives already had about her qualifications for the job. But getting the knowledge was more important to her than her image.

"You piss, moan, and argue that the corpse is on their side or that the crime happened there. You get out a tape measure to prove where the boundary is or who has the bigger dick. You use whatever dirt you have on them, whatever favors they owe you, whatever leverage you've got to make them take the body and the aggravation that comes with it," Duncan said. "But I almost always end up taking the body because I'm a softy."

She took her eyes off the road to give him an incredulous look. "You care that much about some LAPD cop having a bad day?"

"Hell no," Duncan said. "I do it because the victim deserves a cop who will work the case instead of one who is more intent on figuring out how some poor bastard who got shot four times in the back, and got dumped on the jurisdictional line, can be written off as a suicide."

Eve smiled to herself. Maybe she was lucky to get partnered with a guy on his way out who didn't give a damn anymore. At least he had once, and that counted for something. They made an odd-looking couple. He was old and fat and had a creative comb-over to hide his thinning hair. She was young and slim, her brown hair cut into a practical bob. They could be mistaken for a father and daughter who liked to carry Glocks.

At the intersection of Mulholland and Mulholland, there were some houses to the north, a two-story office building on the western corner behind a line of pines, and a wooded patch of oaks to the east that ran through the hillside between a private school and a housing tract.

Eve turned right onto Mulholland Drive, heading southbound, and saw a black-and-white parked behind a pickup truck on the side of the road. An LAPD plain-wrap Crown Vic was parked across the street, facing north. Two detectives leaned against their car, chatting with a uniformed officer. The detectives looked like they'd taken advantage of the "buy one, get one free" sale at Men's Wearhouse and split the cost to get the off-the-rack suits they were wearing.

"The two suits are Detectives Frank Knobb and Arnie Prescott, out of Canoga Park," Duncan said as she parked behind the black-and-white. "Our paths have crossed a few times. Between the two of 'em, they've been around as long as I have."

Eve appreciated that Duncan didn't use the opportunity to mention yet again that she wasn't born when he'd first pinned on his badge.

Duncan got out, hiked up his pants, waited for a car to pass, then crossed the street to speak to the detectives. Eve went over to check out the truck, which was covered with pine needles. The windshield was spattered with blood from the inside and a body was slumped in the driver's seat.

"Hey, Dunkin' Donuts," one of the detectives said as Duncan approached them. "How's it going?"

"Counting the days, Frank," Duncan said. "Another hundred and sixty-three and I'm out of here. Have you heard about my new partner, Detective Ronin?"

The two LAPD detectives looked over at Eve, who was still across the street, studying the truck.

"Deathfist?" Frank Knobb said. "Sure. She's a legend."

Eve was previously a deputy out in Lancaster and unknown to anybody on the LAPD or anywhere else. But four months ago, while off duty, she witnessed actor Blake Largo, who starred as the invincible action hero Deathfist in a globally successful string of movies, assault a woman in a restaurant parking lot. Eve confronted him, he took a swing at her, and she put him on the ground. She pressed his million-dollar face to the pavement until police arrived. A bystander got it all on video with his phone and uploaded it to YouTube. The video got eleven million hits in less than a week. Now everybody called her Deathfist.

So she ignored Knobb's snide remark and focused her attention on the driver of the truck. His head lolled back on the headrest. His throat was slit and the jagged cut gaped open like an obscene, bloody smile. A Rambo knife lay on the passenger seat. She thought it might be a suicide, considering that the knife was right beside him and the largely residential, very safe neighborhood where the victim was found. But if it was suicide, he'd picked an odd place to end his life. The last thing he saw as he bled out was Gelson's, an upscale supermarket. Then again, Gelson's was heaven to some people.

"You're shitting me," Arnie Prescott said, studying Eve. "A viral video is all it takes at the sheriff's department to step up from burglary to homicide?"

It had more to do with the timing of the video, which came out amid revelations that sheriff's deputies were beating prisoners at the county jail. The enormous positive PR she got was a welcome distraction from the scandal and encouraged the embattled sheriff to keep her at the top of the news cycle for as long as possible. He did that by showering her with accolades, which included offering her a promotion. What she wanted was a transfer to Robbery-Homicide and she got it, making her the youngest woman ever in the division. The public and the media loved it. The rank and file at the LASD, primarily the 86 percent of them who had testicles, did not.

"The sheriff's department doesn't have the LAPD's high standards," Knobb said.

"No wonder you're cashing out now," Prescott said to Duncan.

Duncan didn't argue the point. "What's the story on the dead man?"

"A jogger spotted the body and called 911," Knobb said. "The operator called the LAPD. This fine young patrol officer showed up, saw the guy was not merely dead, but most sincerely dead, and brought us in."

"What this officer failed to notice in all the excitement was the boulder." Prescott pointed to the median, where a newly installed boulder sat in a bed of flowers with the words **WELCOME TO CALABASAS** and a soaring bird decoratively carved on its north face. "And which side of the boulder the truck was parked on."

Knobb grinned at Duncan. "Your side."

Sure enough, the truck was parked a few feet south of the invisible city limits line conveniently demarcated by the boulder, putting it in Calabasas. Eve looked at the road on the Los Angeles side and her anger flared. She didn't like being played.

The uniformed officer shrugged sheepishly. "My bad."

"So here you are," Prescott said.

"Lucky us," Duncan said with a weary sigh.

"We stuck around to secure the scene as a professional courtesy," Knobb said.

"Really?" Eve said. The two LAPD detectives looked at her like a naughty child who'd spoken up while the adults were talking. "Because I thought securing the scene meant making sure it wasn't disturbed."

"It doesn't look disturbed to me," Knobb said.

"The truck is covered with pine needles," Eve said. "It obviously spent the night parked under a pine tree, which is odd, since the nearest one is down at the corner in Los Angeles."

Prescott snorted. "You ever heard of wind?"

She stared at the detectives, not bothering to hide the disgust on her face. "So why aren't there any pine needles on the sidewalk or the street around the truck?"

The two detectives maintained eye contact with her but the uniformed officer looked away. Duncan shook his head at the two remorseless detectives.

"It's your case and as a professional courtesy we're not going to tell anybody about this little stunt." Duncan hiked up his pants and shifted his attention to the officer. "But I want you to think about something, son. If forensic issues end up torpedoing their case, do you think these two will have your back or make you the fall guy? I'd protect my ass if I were you."

Duncan walked back across the street and gestured to Eve to follow him back to the car. Eve got into the driver's seat, started up the car, made a U-turn around the median and then a right back onto Mulholland Drive, heading east.

Eve assumed the detectives had pulled rank and ordered the officer to push the truck over the line. The officer's patrol car had welded steel bars on the front bumper that would enable him to move the truck without damaging his own vehicle.

"Who were they trying to screw by moving the body over the line into Calabasas?" Eve asked. "You or me?"

"Let me give you some advice. I know you're used to being the center of attention, but when shit happens to you, it isn't always personal."

"What's that supposed to mean? They intended to screw us."

"No, not us. All Knobb and Prescott knew was that two LASD detectives were going to show up. They didn't know it was going to be the hotshot who didn't deserve her promotion and the old fat ass on his way out the door."

She nodded. "So they're just lazy assholes."

"That's right. It's nothing personal." Duncan reached for the mike and let the dispatcher know that the body was in Los Angeles and that the LAPD was taking the case.

The dispatcher immediately responded with a new call for them, a possible person down at a home on a cul-de-sac in Topanga, which was only a few miles southeast of their current location.

"Reporting party Alexis Ward says the resident failed to show up for work and doesn't answer her phone. The RP looked in a window and saw blood, believes the resident is inside, perhaps injured. 22-Paul-7, fire and paramedics are en route. You're clear code three."

"Copy," Duncan said. "22-David-1 rolling from Mulholland Drive and Topanga Canyon."

# CHAPTER TWO

Topanga Canyon Boulevard was a wooded two-lane road that snaked up into the Santa Monica Mountains, then down alongside a mostly dry creek bed to the Pacific Coast Highway.

For Eve, it was a road into the past. It was a different way of life up there, rustic and isolated, still rooted in the beatnik and hippie cultures of the mid-twentieth century. But that lifestyle was facing extinction as seclusion-seeking celebrities and high-tech millionaires moved in, co-opting the culture as a retro design aesthetic and personal fashion statement, wearing their faux tie-dyed T-shirts as they drove their Bentley convertibles to brunch at the Inn of the Seventh Ray. For airport limo drivers and people who lived in the San Fernando Valley, Topanga Canyon was just a way to get into West LA without using the 405.

Deep into the canyon, she took a left onto a narrow country road with disintegrating asphalt that followed the southern slopes of Topanga State Park. The homes were few and far between, most of them ramshackle bungalows and '70s-era ranch houses with a handful of new gated estates sprinkled among them.

The road ended in a cul-de-sac that abutted a steep wooded hillside. At the end of the court was a poorly maintained, unfenced ranch home with two cars in the driveway—an old Ford Taurus with oxidized paint and a Nissan Sentra. A woman in her early thirties paced anxiously in front of the house.

"She's keyed up," Duncan said as Eve pulled up to the driveway. "You better talk to her, woman-to-woman."

"Good idea, because you know we don't even have to speak to each other," Eve said, putting the car into park. "Our uteruses can communicate telepathically."

"I think the correct term is 'uteri.' "

The two detectives emerged from the car. Duncan took a notebook from his back pocket as they approached the woman. Eve noticed that the notepad was curved by his buttocks.

Eve flashed her badge. "I'm Detective Eve Ronin and this is Detective Duncan Pavone with the Los Angeles County Sheriff's Department. Are you the woman who called 911?"

"Alexis Ward," she said, nodding, her voice cracking just a bit with concern. "You've got to get in there. Something's wrong."

"We will, but we need more information before we can bust in," Eve said. "Who lives here?"

"Tanya Kenworth. That's her Taurus, just like her sign. Mine, too." Alexis touched her necklace. A silver bull's head dangled from the thin chain. "We're astrological sisters, both born in April. I think that's why we became friends the instant we started waitressing together at Rockne's."

"Oh yeah, up on Kanan," Duncan said. "I thought you looked familiar. I go there a lot. They've got great tri-tip."

"Tanya was supposed to pick me up at six this morning to make our seven o'clock call time at Paramount," Alexis said. "She'd never miss that. Never."

"Call time?" Duncan asked, looking up from the notes he was jotting on his pad.

"When we're supposed to be on set for hair and makeup. We're extras on *Grey's Anatomy*. I went to the set on my own but I must've left a hundred voice mail and text messages for her. I came here as soon as we wrapped the scene I was in."

Eve asked: "Does Tanya live here alone?"

"She's got two kids, Caitlin and Troy," Alexis said. "They're ten and seven. This is her boyfriend's house, but she's moving out as soon as she can find a place."

Eve felt the muscles in her shoulder tighten up, a common reaction to stress, specifically the kind caused by her mother. This house was a dead ringer for her childhood home in Encino and Tanya sounded just like her mom, a single mother on the fringes of Hollywood trying to raise three kids. She rolled her shoulders to loosen them up. "Does he know that?"

"Oh yeah," she said. "It got ugly. That's why I

was worried when I couldn't reach her. What if he hurt her? What if she's inside there right now, bleeding to death, while we're out here talking?"

The pitch of Alexis' voice increased as she spoke and Eve held up her hands in a halting gesture to calm her down. "Okay, okay, wait right here. We'll go check things out. You told the 911 operator that you peeked in the kitchen window and saw blood. Where was that?"

"Back of the house," Alexis said.

At that moment, a sheriff's department patrol car rolled up behind their Explorer and two uniformed deputies, Tom Ross and Eddie Clayton, got out. Ross was an ex-marine and everything about his body language screamed military. He could be dressed as Santa Claus and it wouldn't fool anyone. People called Clayton "Shades" because he almost never took off his wraparound sunglasses.

Duncan waved them over. "Stay with Ms. Ward, will you? The fire department will be here in a minute. Tell 'em to sit tight."

Eve and Duncan walked into the backyard. Some rusting lawn furniture, a deflated soccer ball, and a torn standing umbrella were strewn amid the dead grass and weeds.

"My mom was an extra," Eve said, surprising herself by volunteering the information to Duncan. "They're human set dressing, decoration like a couch or a potted plant. The thing is, they're hoping to be discovered by somebody when their job is not to attract any attention at all."

"Was your mother discovered?"

"Nope," Eve said as they approached the door and the kitchen window. "But she still hasn't given up hope."

Eve and Duncan peeked in the window, which was over the sink, and saw a pool of blood in the center of the yellowed linoleum floor. Bloody drag marks ran out into the hallway.

"Shit," Duncan said.

She looked at him. "Exigent circumstances?"

In the absence of a search warrant, in order to enter the house they needed credible grounds to believe that immediate action was necessary to save a person's life, prevent evidence from being destroyed, or stop a suspect from escaping.

"Exigent as it gets," Duncan said.

Both of the detectives drew their guns. He gestured to her to take the lead. She tested the doorknob. It was locked. She took a step back and kicked the door open.

The first thing Eve noticed was the strange smell. She'd been expecting the oddly metallic scent of blood. Instead, the odor evoked the ridiculous image in her mind of an over-chlorinated swimming pool in a mechanic's garage. It didn't make sense. But she couldn't think about that now.

She cleared her mind and moved into the kitchen, careful not to step in any of the bloody smears. Duncan moved off to one side, his eyes on the hallway, and gestured her forward with a nod of his head.

"Police," Eve shouted. "Is anybody here?"

The house was quiet, the air still, in sharp contrast to the story of violence illustrated in blood on the floor and in the spatter she saw on the cupboards. But the dark energy generated by the violence was gone. Now all she felt was the emptiness, the vacancy of anything living besides her and Duncan.

Duncan took a covering position as Eve edged around the doorway into the hall. The shag carpet was soaked with blood and there were crimson streaks on the wall. The story was getting more horrific with each step they took.

"This is the police," Eve said loudly and firmly. "If there's anybody in this house, you need to come out now, hands in the air."

Nobody appeared. The only sound Eve heard was her own breathing.

Eve and Duncan shared grim looks and moved slowly into the living room. The front door was spattered with blood and two children's backpacks were lying in dried puddles of blood on the floor. Eve felt a pang of fear in her chest for the children. She hoped that they were in school or at a friend's house. Anywhere but here.

"Tanya, Caitlin, Troy, if you're hiding, it's safe to come out now," Eve said. "We're the police. You're safe with us."

The house remained deathly quiet. The only people moving here were the two of them. But that didn't mean they were alone.

She scanned the rest of the room. There was a bed pillow, a blanket, and a sheet on the couch, which faced a flat-screen TV that was way too big for the room. A small dog bed, with a chewed-up Nylabone in it, was against one wall. Where was the dog?

Eve turned and looked back down the hall, where trails of blood led into three different doorways. Flies were coming into the house now, buzzing loudly past her ears. She looked at Duncan and he nodded. Eve followed one of the blood trails into a bedroom while Duncan went into the bedroom across the hall.

She stood in the doorway, taking in the pink walls and the blood spatter on the shelves of dolls and stuffed animals. Eve moved into the room, eased around the blood-soaked carpet, and bumped into a standing electric fan, nearly knocking it over. She crouched down and peered under the bed. The lifeless eyes of a stuffed bear stared back at her.

Eve rose, crossed the room, and opened the sliding mirrored closet door with the toe of her foot. A young girl's clothes hung from the rod, including a princess gown, probably from Halloween. Eve's sister, Lisa, three years younger than her, once had a costume like that.

"Clear," Eve shouted and went back to the hall.

Duncan emerged from what appeared to be Troy's room. There were toy cars on the floor and Marvel superhero posters on the walls. Eve's little brother, Kenny, five years younger than her, liked superheroes, too, when he was a kid. But only the DC ones like Superman and Batman.

"Clear," Duncan said.

They moved in unison, following a blood trail to the next open doorway. It was the bathroom and there was blood everywhere, as if someone had heaved buckets of it into the room, especially in the bathtub. Every surface was splashed or spattered with blood, even the ceiling.

Eve's own blood went cold, chilling her from the inside out, goose bumps rising on her flesh. The flies had found the room, too, and their buzzing seemed amplified, as if channeled through loudspeakers, but she knew it was all in her head.

There were blood-soaked dish sponges and several blood-smeared bottles of Clorox on the counter and in the sink. The smell of cleanser and motor oil was overpowering and, combined with the bloody tableau, repulsive. She fought her gag reflex, willing her muscles to relax. She would not humiliate herself, and contaminate the crime scene, by vomiting.

"My God," Duncan said.

Somehow hearing his shaky voice was reassuring and helped her maintain control. He was as disturbed by this as she was.

They backed away from the bathroom and eyed the two remaining doors, both ajar, both at the end of blood trails on the carpet. Eve took the door on the left and Duncan took the one on the right.

Eve stepped into the master bedroom. The bedding was missing from the king-size bed, the blood-soaked mattress was hacked to shreds, and the headboard was speckled with blood. She crouched down, peered under the bed, saw nothing but a pair of women's slippers and a small marijuana pipe, then moved to the closet, nudging it open with her shoe. It was filled with clothes, belonging to a man and woman, but nobody was inside.

"Clear," Eve said and returned to the hallway.

The other door was open to the garage. Duncan came back in, holstering his weapon.

"The garage is empty, but there are some drops of blood leading to where a car must have been parked."

Eve swallowed back some bile and cleared her throat. "Have you ever seen anything like this before?"

Duncan shook his head. "Thanks a lot."

"What's that supposed to mean?"

"If we'd taken the dead guy in the truck, Crockett and Tubbs would have got this call," Duncan said, referring to the other team of homicide detectives at the station. "But you had to point out the pine needles."

Duncan marched back to the kitchen and out into the backyard, where he stopped to get some fresh air. Eve followed him out and stood beside him, neither of them visible to the deputies, Alexis Ward, or anybody else in the cul-de-sac.

After a long moment, Duncan spoke again. "There's going to be a shitload of desk work and legwork on this case."

"Yeah, I get it," Eve said, irritated. "The other case would have been a lot less trouble."

"That's not what I meant. I'll take the desk, you take the street."

She looked at him. "You're the senior detective. You should take the lead."

"I just did by dividing the workload."

It took her a second to figure out his angle. "You're making me the face of the investigation."

"And the first set of eyes," he said. "My sight isn't so good anymore. I missed those pine needles, didn't I?"

"That's not it," she said. "What's the real reason you're putting me in the spotlight?"

He sighed and glanced back at the house. "This

case is going to get very big and very ugly very fast. It won't make or break my career, and I sure as hell don't need more nightmares to take with me into retirement."

He was telling her, honestly and directly, that he was done. Eve respected him for that and didn't blame him for his decision. He'd put in his time. It was going to be her neck and soul on the line from now on.

"Okay," she said.

"I'll call in CSU and get a warrant started," Duncan said. "You should find out what you can about the kids and the boyfriend."

She nodded. The enormity of what she was taking on was beginning to sink in and it left her momentarily at a loss for words. Something awful had happened in that house and it was going to be her job to find out what it was, seek some measure of justice, and live with the horrors that were revealed.

She took a deep breath, put on her best poker face, and walked with Duncan to the front of the house.

# CHAPTER THREE

An ambulance and fire truck had arrived and the first responders were standing around, waiting for instructions.

Alexis ran up to Eve. "What's wrong? Is she in there?"

"Nope," Eve said. "The house is empty."

"What did you see?"

"Same thing you did," Eve said. Alexis looked relieved, but that was only because she hadn't seen all the blood beyond the kitchen.

"So where's Tanya?"

"I don't know," Eve said, feeling guilty. Nothing that she'd said to Alexis was a lie but it was all misleading. "Excuse me for a moment."

Eve went over to the ambulance crew and the firemen. "You can go. There's nobody home."

She turned to Deputies Ross and Clayton, making sure her back was to Alexis and Duncan, and lowered her voice to a near whisper. "Call in two more units. Freeze the scene. Nobody goes in or out except CSU."

They nodded their understanding and she went back to Alexis and Duncan, who had his curled pad out again and was making notes.

"Where do Caitlin and Troy go to school?" he asked.

"Canyon Oaks Elementary," she said.

Duncan glanced at Eve. He had what he needed to work with.

"Where is their father?" Eve asked, taking over questioning and giving Duncan an out to go back to their SUV to start making calls.

"Up in Merced. His name is Cleve Kenworth. He and Tanya divorced a few years ago. She doesn't talk about him."

Eve took out her pad from the inside pocket of her navy-blue Ann Taylor blazer, one of three in the same style, but in different colors, that she bought online when she got her detective shield and hung up her uniform. "What do you know about Tanya's boyfriend?"

The ambulance and fire trucks began backing out of the cul-de-sac and that seemed to give Alexis some reassurance that things were going to be okay. Eve could see Alexis relaxing, her body loosening up.

"He's an asshole," Alexis said.

"Let's start with his name and his job and work our way up to the asshole part," Eve said.

Alexis smiled, more evidence to Eve that she was calming down. "Jared Rawlins. He's a grip. One of the guys who moves lights and carries stuff on movie sets."

Eve knew what a grip was. Her sister's father was a grip who dated their mother for a few weeks. He came around to see Lisa at Christmas and on her birthday for a few years, then disappeared from their lives. Eve remembered his freckled face and calloused hands and that he was nice. He had brought all three kids See's caramel lollipops when he came to visit Lisa.

"What show is he on?" Eve asked.

"He's a day player. Something different all the time. Does a lot of stuff. Movies, TV series, commercials, videos, an occasional porno."

"What makes him an asshole?"

"The way he talks to Tanya, always putting her down. He hates the kids, too. He calls them rats like he's joking, but he's not."

Eve's father was like that. A journeyman TV director who never married but had fathered a lot of children, all with aspiring actresses and production assistants, and rarely paid a dime of child support. The few times Eve saw him during her early childhood was when her mother would bring her to family court in an effort to influence the judge. Now her dad lived in a bungalow at the Motion Picture and Television Country House and Hospital in Woodland Hills, not even five miles from her condo or where she worked, but she'd never visited him.

"Where's Jack Shit?" Alexis asked, breaking into Eve's thoughts.

"Excuse me?" Eve said.

"Their dog. An old Jack Russell terrier–shih tzu mix. He barks at everything. Did you see him?"

"No, we didn't." Eve had forgotten about the empty dog bed in the living room.

"That makes no sense," Alexis said, stiffening up again. "They'd never let Jack Shit out of the house off leash. He'd be coyote bait."

"I'll look into that." Eve waved to Deputy Clayton to come over and faced Alexis again. "Thank you for everything, Ms. Ward. Please give the deputy your contact information before you go home. We'll be in touch as soon as we know something."

Eve left Alexis with Clayton and went over to her SUV, where Duncan sat in the passenger seat holding a cell phone to his ear.

"I'm on hold waiting to talk to the ADA about the warrant," he said. "CSU is on the way and I had dispatch send a patrol unit to Canyon Oaks to check on the kids. What did you learn?"

"The boyfriend's name is Jared Rawlins. He's a grip. Maybe his union can tell us where he's working."

"If he's working," Duncan said. "Could be he's in the wind."

"Her ex-husband's name is Cleve and he lives up in Merced," Eve said. All she knew about Merced was that it was a small town in central California, 275 miles north of Los Angeles. She'd never been there.

"I'll contact Merced PD and get them to track him down," Duncan said.

"The family dog is missing, too. Maybe it ran off when whatever happened in the house went down. Do you think we can get animal control to look for him?"

He looked at her, straight-faced. "Sure thing, they search for lost dogs all the time. That's what they do."

"You're being sarcastic," she said.

"They'd only look for it if it was rabid, and even then I'm not so sure. What do you think we'd get from the dog anyway?"

"Jack Shit," she said.

"That's right."

"That's the dog's name. Jack Shit. He's a Jack Russell terrier–shih tzu mix."

"Adorable," Duncan said.

Eve knew that there was nothing to be gained from finding the dog. She just didn't like the idea of it being some coyote's dinner.

"I'll secure the scene for CSU," she said.

She went to the rear of the Explorer, opened the back, took out a big roll of yellow CRIME SCENE tape from the trunk, and walked back to the house. She tied one end of the tape to a streetlight and walked the perimeter of the property, stopping every now and then to secure the tape around a tree, bush, lawn chair, or other object. As she walked, she kept her eyes open for anything out of the ordinary.

It made her look busy while giving her an

excuse to think about what she was taking on. Most of her investigative experience was in home and business burglaries. The few homicides that she'd worked were hardly big mysteries. One was an elderly man who killed his Alzheimer's-afflicted wife, then himself. Another was a homeless man who stabbed another homeless man in a dispute over scavenging rights to a dumpster behind a grocery store. This case was more complex than anything she'd tackled before.

But what did she know? Only that a woman was missing and that some terrible violence had seemingly occurred in her house. There were no bodies. So was she dealing with a murder? Multiple murders? An abduction? It was way too soon to tell.

Eve was in the backyard when she noticed a depression in the dry brush going from the dead lawn up into the grove of trees at the top of the hill. Someone, or some animal, had trampled through the weeds recently. Perhaps it was the trail left by the dog when it fled the house.

She set down the roll of tape on a lawn chair and trudged up the hillside, creating a parallel path alongside the one that was already there so she wouldn't contaminate any possible evidence. The dirt was hard and the weeds were like hay.

She stepped up into the trees and was surprised to see a rumpled sleeping bag on the ground surrounded by trash from a McDonald's takeout meal. The sleeping bag wasn't soiled, dirty, or covered with leaves. She squatted beside the trash and looked at a pickle slice in a Big Mac carton. The pickle was still moist.

This campsite hadn't been here long. Maybe a day at most.

She looked back the way she came. Whoever was here had a clear view of Tanya's house, front yard, and the cul-de-sac. She could see the Crime Scene Unit van arriving. Had somebody been watching the house? If so, why and for how long? Did whoever it was have something to do with Tanya's disappearance and the violence? If not, did he see what happened?

She was about to start taking pictures with her phone when a twig snapped behind her. She whirled around and at the same instant some rampaging hairy monster—a grizzly bear? a werewolf?—burst out of the trees and whacked her across the head with a rock.

She felt a blinding explosion of pain and fell on her side. The enraged beast kicked her hard in the stomach, forcing the air out of her lungs. She couldn't breathe and instinctively curled into a fetal position, protecting her midsection.

The beast kicked her in the head and everything went dark.

# CHAPTER FOUR

Eve opened her eyes, cheek to the ground, her vision blurred, and immediately sucked in air, drawing in some dirt along with it. She coughed, breathed deeply again, and unfurled herself, her vision sharpening on a bit of chopped white onion just beyond her nose. Her head throbbed and it hurt to breathe, but she didn't think she had any broken ribs.

Her gun was pressing painfully against her side, pinned between her and the ground, but it was a good pain. It meant that whoever struck her hadn't taken her weapon and wasn't going to shoot her or somebody else with it.

She sat up slowly, slightly dizzy. The sleeping bag and trash were gone and so was whoever, or whatever, had attacked her. No, it was a whoever. She didn't believe in monsters, despite what she saw.

Or thought she saw.

Eve looked back down at the cul-de-sac. The CSU team was just emerging from their van, so she'd been out for only a minute or two. Bracing herself on a pine tree for support, she rose unsteadily to her feet. She touched the side of her head, above her right temple, where she'd been hit with the rock and kicked. Her hair was wet

37

and when she lowered her hand, she saw blood on her fingertips.

Shit.

She glanced around and spotted a rock a foot away with fresh blood on a sharp edge. He could have caved her head in with it but didn't. She was lucky to be alive.

Eve took a deep breath and, still shaky, started back down the hill, immediately lost her footing, and slid on her ass for a few feet. She sat still for a moment, feeling stupid, then got up slowly, brushed the dirt and weeds off herself, and tried going down the hill again, more carefully this time.

She got down to the backyard without stumbling and headed for the Explorer. Duncan got out of the passenger seat when he spotted her and met her halfway.

"What the hell happened to you?" he said.

She knew how awful she looked. Her head was bleeding and her clothes were dirty. She wasn't off to a great start as a lead detective. But she pressed on as if she was oblivious to it. Maybe that would make him ignore it, too.

"I was looking around up on the hill and came across a sleeping bag and some trash," she said and kept walking, Duncan keeping pace beside her. "Before I could take any pictures, someone hit me from behind and ran off with the stuff."

"Did you get a look at him?"

She wasn't going to tell him about the hairy beast. It was a crazy story that would go viral around the station and undermine any chance she'd ever have of establishing credibility.

"No," she said, and reached into the Explorer's passenger door pocket for one of the napkins Duncan always kept there. He spilled a lot of stuff on himself.

Duncan tipped his head toward the hill. "That's Topanga State Park. It's crawling with the homeless. They can be fiercely protective about their things. He probably didn't realize you were a cop."

"Whoever it was had a clear view of the house." She dabbed a napkin against her wound. The napkin came back red. "We need to talk to him."

"I'll send CSU up there to see what evidence they can find and I'll get the park rangers to look for a guy in a hurry lugging a sleeping bag."

"Tell the CSU guys that the blood on the rock is mine."

He squinted at her head. "That's a nasty cut. You need to go to the ER."

"The hell with that." Eve balled up the napkin, stuffed it in her pocket, and went to the back of the SUV. She raised the tailgate, found her LASD baseball cap, and gently placed it on her head, neatly hiding the blood in her hair. "There, all better."

Duncan stared at her. She stared back at him. It felt like an ax was cleaving her skull apart.

"What?" she said. "Are you going to tell me how often people who suffer head injuries but don't see a doctor afterwards die hours later from subdural hematomas?"

"I have no idea what you're talking about," Duncan said. "What I've got to tell you is that Tanya's kids didn't show up for school today."

She looked back at the house, thought about the two backpacks left by the door, and was filled with dread.

# CHAPTER FIVE

A half hour later, Eve and Duncan were still waiting on a warrant authorizing the CSU team to enter the house. There were two CSU techs up on the hill—the other four were laying down a paper carpet between the sidewalk and the kitchen door in preparation for going in.

Eve's headache had ebbed and she could feel that the baseball cap was stuck to the dried blood in her hair. She was antsy to get something done, so she gathered the half dozen uniformed deputies at her SUV and addressed them as a group.

"I need you to talk to the neighbors along the road. I know this house is isolated, but there's still a chance that somebody saw or heard something. Also go to all of the trailheads for the Topanga State Park, take down license numbers, makes, and models of any cars that are parked there, and talk to any hikers who come back, ask them if they saw anything. Hold any guy you see carrying a sleeping bag." She looked back at Duncan, who sat in the SUV, the air-conditioning running, his door open a crack. "Did I miss anything?"

"You covered it all," he said. Then his phone buzzed. He answered it.

"Okay," she said to the deputies. "You've got your jobs. Bring your reports to me at the station."

The deputies nodded and headed off. A CSU tech in a Tyvek jumpsuit and booties approached Eve from the backyard. He was tall, very thin, and his Adam's apple was so big he looked like he was trying to swallow a baseball. His name was Lou Noomis and he was one of the two techs who'd gone up the hill.

"Find anything up there?" she asked.

"Not really. I took some pictures and collected these." Noomis held up an evidence baggie containing dirt with one hand and another baggie with chips of bark in the other.

"What for?" she asked.

"I smelled urine on the base of a tree. So I took a sample of the bark and dirt for the DNA."

"How do you know it's human pee and not animal pee?"

"They smell different."

He started to bring the bags to her to sniff but she shooed him away. "I'll take your word for it."

Duncan got out of the SUV and pocketed his phone. "We've got a warrant."

Eve, Duncan, and the CSU techs put Tyvek shoe covers over their footwear and rubber gloves on their hands.

Nan Baker, the large African American woman in her forties who led the CSU, pulled the hood of her Tyvek suit over her hair, picked up her bag, and led the way down the paper carpet like a general going into battle.

Eve went into the kitchen more slowly this time, paying closer attention to the details she missed on her first visit. The kitchen hadn't been updated in twenty years. The appliances were old and the countertops were granite tiles. She noticed an array of magnets on the front of the refrigerator. The magnets were from Domino's, Mr. Plunger, a gardener, and other restaurants and services and held artwork by the kids, a school calendar, and discount coupons. A CSU tech stationed himself in the kitchen and began taking pictures of the blood.

There was a purse on the floor that looked as if it had been dropped. Some of the contents—a roll of lip balm and a tiny bottle of Purell—had spilled out. Eve crouched beside the purse and used her pen to peek inside.

"No cell phone. No house keys." She teased out a key chain with a Ford logo from the purse and dangled it on the end of her pen. "But the car keys are here."

The CSU tech held out an open baggie to Eve. "Saves us the trouble of breaking into her car."

Eve dropped the keys in the bag, stood up, and followed Duncan into the living room.

Another CSU tech was photographing every-thing. Duncan stopped and stared at the puddle of blood and the backpacks and she knew what he was thinking: the children were either gravely injured or dead.

Eve went to Caitlin's room and found Nan leaning close to a row of Barbie dolls that sat on the edge of a shelf, their legs crossed, blood spattered on their happy plastic faces.

"What's your initial impression?" Eve asked.

Nan straightened up and answered without looking at her. "People died here."

"How many?"

"Certainly more than one, based on the amount of blood I can see, particularly the spatter patterns on the walls, indicating blunt force trauma or arterial spray, and multiple, deep saturation stains on the carpets indicating catastrophic blood loss. Come back in a few hours and ask me again." Nan looked at her now. "We're going to be here processing this scene for a long time."

"How long is long?"

"A couple of days at least."

Someone outside called Eve's name. She turned and went back through the kitchen and out into the yard, where Deputy Ross was waiting for her on the grass.

"A guy just showed up in a truck, says he lives here," Ross said. "His name is Jared Rawlins."

Duncan joined Eve. "What's up?"

"The boyfriend is here," Eve said, not sure

how to handle this new development. He was an obvious suspect, given what they'd learned about him from Alexis, but if he was responsible for whatever violence had happened here, it was pretty ballsy of him to show up at the scene as it was being processed. She decided to let Jared's demeanor and Duncan's body language guide her tactics.

Eve and Duncan peeled off their gloves and followed Deputy Ross back out to the cul-de-sac, where Deputy Clayton was standing in front of a dirt-caked Ford F-150 pickup, preventing it from going to the house. The man in the driver's seat had a deep tan, a day's growth of beard, and a military buzz cut to compensate for a receding hairline.

Duncan approached the driver's side window, which was rolled down. "Mr. Rawlins? I'm Detective Pavone and this is Detective Ronin."

"What the hell is going on? What are you doing in my house?"

"Step out of the truck and we can discuss it," Duncan said.

Jared sighed, shut off his truck, and got out. Eve looked him over. He was a muscled man and spent a lot of time outdoors. His tank top and cargo shorts were faded and his chest and arms were as tan as his face and neck. There was dirt caked on his work boots.

"Now are you going to tell me what the fuck is

45

going on here?" Jared said. "Why can't I go in my own house?"

His anger didn't make sense to Eve. "Have you got a reason to be ticked off, Mr. Rawlins?"

"Wouldn't you be if you came home to a bunch of cops who wouldn't let you in your house?"

"No," Eve said. "The first thing I'd want to know is if Tanya and the kids are okay."

"Why? She's at work and the kids are at school. The problem here is that something is happening in *my house* and I'm not being told what it is or let inside."

His anger was making a little more sense to Eve. The house had become a battleground for him, first with Tanya and now with the police. He wanted to assert his authority over what was his. The question Eve had now was how far he'd gone to assert it.

"Tanya is not at work and the kids aren't in school," Duncan said. "They're all missing."

"*That's* what this big production is about?" Jared laughed. "Jesus. It's nothing."

"What makes you so sure?" Eve said.

"Because she's a flake. She could've woken up this morning, looked at the big blue sky, and decided, 'Hey, it's a beach day. I'll just blow off everything and hit the sand with the kids.' That's her. Whoever called you freaked out over nothing."

"She freaked out over the blood," Eve said.

46

"Blood?"

"It's all over the place, Mr. Rawlins," Duncan said. "It looks like a butcher shop in there."

Jared stared at them for a long moment, studying their faces, adding something up in his mind. "You said Tanya and the kids are gone, right?"

"And the dog, too," Eve said.

"So it's just blood," Jared said.

Duncan cocked his head, studying Jared now. "Just blood?"

"Look, we're having some problems. I told her to move out. Maybe this is payback. Maybe she went batshit, tossed a bucket of pig blood all over the place, and hit the road."

"That seems extreme," Eve said.

"She's an actress, or at least she thinks she is. She turns everything into a major drama. She'd love all this attention."

Eve couldn't reject the possibility that he was right, but the spatter told her a tale of violence that wouldn't emerge from somebody simply splashing the blood around the house. And she had a hard time believing that Tanya would paint with the blood to create the impression of a terrible struggle.

Even so, Eve forced herself to keep an open mind to all possibilities. Making any assumptions this early in the investigation could lead to tunnel vision that would prevent her from spotting any evidence that didn't reinforce her preconceptions. That was especially dangerous in the initial hours of an investigation. She'd learned that from books, not experience.

Duncan took his pad out of his back pocket and clicked his ballpoint pen for action. "When was the last time you saw her and the kids?"

"Tuesday night, before I went to bed. I left the house at three a.m. I had to get to Lancaster to start rigging the lights on a Kevin Costner western that's being shot in the desert."

"And you're just getting back now?" Eve said. It was Thursday afternoon.

"I was bushed after shooting so I spent the night in a motel. To be honest, I was looking forward to a big bed. I'm tired of sleeping on the couch."

"It's your house," Duncan said. "Why isn't Tanya on the couch?"

"Because I'm a fucking gentleman."

Eve saw that as an opening and took it. "Then you won't mind being a gentleman and coming over to the Lost Hills station to answer some more questions for us."

"Sure," Jared said.

Duncan said, "How about letting us take a look at your truck?"

Jared dug the keys out of his pocket and handed them to Duncan. "No reason not to."

"Thanks, we appreciate it." Duncan tossed the keys to Deputy Ross, who caught them. "The deputy will give you a consent form to fill out and sign authorizing us to search your vehicle. When you're done with that, we'll give you a ride to the station."

"Will you throw in a wash?" Jared asked, amused with himself.

"It's a search," Duncan said. "Not a detailing."

Jared shrugged and swaggered off with the deputy to a patrol car to fill out the form. Eve and Duncan watched him go.

"I didn't spot any suspicious cuts or bruises on his arms or legs that might indicate that he was in a struggle," Eve said.

"Yeah, it was real nice of him to wear a tank top and shorts so we could see that."

"It's what grips wear," she said. "They do a lot of work outdoors."

"It was also mighty convenient that he was on an out-of-town shoot while somebody was getting killed in his house."

She was going to argue that, technically, they didn't know that anybody was dead, but then she remembered what Nan said.

*People died here.*

"You think he's responsible," Eve said.

"The fucking gentlemen usually are."

# CHAPTER SIX

The Lost Hills sheriff's station was on Agoura Road, which ran alongside the southern edge of the 101 freeway and straddled the dividing line between the small cities of Agoura and Calabasas.

Eve led Jared down the hall to one of the interrogation rooms. "Can I get you a Coke or something, Mr. Rawlins?"

"Yeah, a Coke would be good, and a Snickers or Milky Way if you've got it. I'm starving."

"I'll see what we've got." She pulled out a seat at the table for him. "Make yourself comfortable and we'll be right back."

Eve stepped out of the room, leaving the door open, and joined Duncan in the hallway, out of Jared's sight and earshot.

"You interview him," Duncan said. "I'll check his alibi."

"Sure," Eve said. The two of them headed for the squad room and they nearly collided with Captain Moffett.

He was in his forties and wore his uniform with so much starch that Eve imagined it was like wearing cardboard. The rigidity suited his personality. He'd recently replaced a captain who was fired for sexually harassing a female deputy, who'd since quit and filed a $2 million lawsuit against the department.

"I was just about to call you," Moffett said to Duncan. "CSU asked for additional resources to process the crime scene you're working. They've never seen so much Goddamn blood."

"Neither have I, Captain," Duncan said.

It went without saying that Eve hadn't, either, not that the captain cared. He ignored her, which had been his standard approach to her since the day he'd paired her with Duncan.

"Is there anything you need?" Moffett asked Duncan.

"A search party and some dogs to check out the woods around the house for bodies."

"Let's put a hold on search parties for now," Moffett said. "It will draw too much attention and sends the wrong message."

"Which is what, sir?" Eve said.

Moffett nailed her with a hard stare. "That the family is dead and we don't know shit." He shifted his gaze back to Duncan. "Keep me updated."

The captain walked away. Duncan shook his head at Eve.

"Congratulations, I think you scored some big points by questioning his orders."

"I just want to understand his reasoning."

"You don't need to," Duncan said. "Your job is to salute and obey."

"That's not it," she said. "He doesn't like me because I was forced on him."

"You were forced on all of us," Duncan said. "Not everyone is as cheerful about it as I am."

"Only because they aren't retiring."

Duncan went into the squad room, which was crammed full of cubicles and file cabinets. There was a vending machine, a microwave oven, a small refrigerator, and some bulk-size boxes of granola bars, coffee sweetener, and breakfast cereal on a table in a corner. He was headed for his cubicle, and Eve was about to go to the food, when they were met by Detectives Wally Biddle and Stan Garvey, known around the station as Crockett and Tubbs.

"I heard you caught a bloody one, Donuts," Biddle said. He colored his hair beach-boy blond and liked to dress in designer clothes that he bought on the cheap at the outlet mall in Camarillo. He was an LA native who'd dreamed of being a competitive surfer and was good at it, just not good enough to go pro.

Duncan glanced at Eve. "Crockett and Tubbs don't know how close they came to getting the case. You owe us one, boys."

Eve continued on to the vending machine while Biddle and Garvey trailed Duncan to his cubicle.

"How about we make your day?" Garvey said. He was black and embraced the Tubbs nickname. He often talked about leaving the job to become a producer. A lot of Hollywood elite lived in Malibu, Hidden Hills, and Calabasas and being assigned to Lost Hills put him in their orbit. In his off-duty time, he worked security at celebrity parties and on studio location shoots. Eve was certain that Garvey wouldn't have arrested Deathfist if he'd been in her place.

"Tell the captain you want to step aside and we'll take the case off your hands," Biddle said.

Eve was plugging coins into the vending machine and could hear every word they were saying. The squad room wasn't that big.

"Why would you want to do that?" Duncan settled into his seat, which squeaked under his weight.

"Out of respect for you," Garvey said. "Deathfist can't hack it and you've done your time. You're almost out the door. You should be taking it easy."

"You shouldn't have to do the work of two detectives," Biddle added.

"I won't be," Duncan said. "She will."

Eve bent down to pull a Coke can out of the vending machine and it aggravated her bruised stomach, the unexpected pain making her wince. She straightened up, took two granola bars from the bulk-size Nature Valley box, and headed back to Duncan's cubicle as Biddle and Garvey were walking away.

She waited until they were gone to ask: "Did

you say that because you have confidence in my energy and ability or because you don't give a shit anymore?"

"Both," Duncan said.

*Fair enough,* she thought. She went to her cubicle, opened her desk drawer, and found her container of Aleve, a twelve-hour pain reliever that she kept for menstrual cramps. She figured it would work just as well on a beating and dry-swallowed a pill.

She returned to the interrogation room, set the Coke and granola bars on the table in front of Jared, and sat down across from him. "We didn't have any candy bars. Hope these will do."

"Thanks," Jared said and popped the tab on the Coke.

Eve took out her notepad and pen. "How did you and Tanya meet?"

He took a sip of his drink. "It was a couple of years ago. She'd just come down here from Merced. I was day-playing on *CSI* and she was a corpse. Best role she's had so far. No lines but plenty of close-ups."

"When did you move in together?"

"Almost immediately. She was living in a crappy one-bedroom apartment in Van Nuys with the kids and couldn't afford babysitters." Jared reached for a granola bar, tore the wrapper open with his teeth, and eased out the bar. "So all of us staying at my place was the only way the two of us could be together, if you know what I mean." He winked at her. "It worked for a while."

"What went wrong?"

He took a bite of his bar and chewed it while he thought about that.

"I hardly saw her between my job and her waitressing and scrounging for acting work. I ended up stuck at home all the time babysitting her unruly kids and Jack Shit. Perfect name for the stinking dog. I was also paying most of the bills. I'd become her sugar daddy with none of the benefits and all of the headaches. So I gave her thirty days to leave."

"How long ago was that?"

"Two months ago." He washed down his granola bar with some more Coke.

"It must be frustrating that she's still there." She wasn't really sympathizing with his problems. Her sympathies were with Caitlin and Troy. The tension in the house must have been hell on the kids, who were stuck with a mom who was hardly there and her boyfriend who resented them. It would have fallen on Caitlin to manage the situation for herself and her brother. Eve knew what that was like, except she had two siblings to watch over. It had often felt to Eve like her mom was just another child under her care, too, only a lot more difficult to control. She wondered if Caitlin felt the same way about Tanya.

"I'd like my bed back, I'll tell you that," Jared said. "The couch is killing me."

"Was Tanya making any effort to go?"

"She told me the other night that she'd found a Realtor to help her out," Jared said. "They were going to meet yesterday after Tanya's Pilates class."

"When is the class?"

"It's at nine, the place by the Topanga post office."

Eve nodded, taking notes. She knew the place. "Do you know who the Realtor is?"

"No, just that it was some lady she met at Pilates."

Eve decided to go in a different direction. "What can you tell me about Tanya's ex-husband?"

"Cleve? I've never met him." Jared used his teeth to tear open the wrapper on the second granola bar. "He sees the kids on holidays. They do the swap at a McDonald's off the freeway in Bakersfield, halfway between Merced and LA. Tanya doesn't bring me along, which is fine by me. I can have a play day."

"Do you remember the name of the hotel you were at last night?" It was a sharp change of subject, one intended to throw him a little off balance, but it didn't work.

"I can do better than that." Jared reached into his pocket, pulled out a folded piece of paper, and slid it across the table to Eve. "My receipt."

She unfolded the paper and looked at the information. It showed him renting a room at a Holiday Inn Express at 7:00 p.m. on Wednesday and checking out at 10:00 a.m. the next morning. Lancaster was in the Mojave Desert, seventy miles north of Los Angeles. It was about a ninety-minute drive from Topanga in typical traffic, but the trip could be made in a little over an hour off peak and with a heavy foot on the gas pedal. She knew that because she'd been stationed out there before transferring to Lost Hills after the YouTube video went viral. Law enforcement in Lancaster was handled by the LASD.

"Can anybody vouch for you being in the room last night?"

Jared smirked and shook his head. "You think I got a room, drove back here, did something awful to Tanya and the kids, and went back to the hotel in time to check out? What kind of asshole do you think I am?"

She could make a list, but instead she just shrugged. "It's my job to think the worst of people. Convince me that you aren't that kind of asshole."

His smirk became a smile. "Ask Jen. She can confirm that we never left the room."

Her mother's name was Jen, short for Jennifer. It was yet another unwelcome personal parallel to the case and it hurt, though Eve didn't know why and she sure as hell wouldn't be analyzing herself to figure it out. She'd just push past it, the way she did with any pain, emotional or physical.

"Does Jen have a last name?"

"I'm sure she does. I don't know it, but I can find out for you. She's a set decorator on the movie," Jared said. "I wasn't cheating on Tanya. We split up weeks ago and a man has legitimate needs."

Eve tore a piece of paper from her notebook and slid the paper and pen across the table to Jared.

"I'd appreciate it if you'd write down any places that Tanya goes to regularly. Gyms, acting classes, that kind of thing. Also, I'd like the names and addresses of any of her friends or family that you know. While you do that, I'll see if we're done with your truck and get you a ride home if we are. Want another Coke or anything?"

"No thanks," he said. "I'm good."

"Back in a minute. The bathroom is across the hall if you need it." Eve closed her notebook, picked up the receipt, and left the room.

# CHAPTER SEVEN

Eve dragged a chair over to Duncan's cubicle and sat down beside his desk. Duncan was eating a sugar donut and looking at a photograph tacked on his wall of the desert view from the backyard of his Palm Springs condo. He spent weekends and holidays there and was planning to make it his permanent home once he retired. Duncan looked like he longed to be there right now.

"How's it going with the fucking gentleman?" Duncan asked.

"Jared doesn't seem the least bit concerned about Tanya or the kids, which is weird. He may just be glad to have them out of the house."

"What was his problem with them?"

"He was tired of paying her bills and taking care of the kids. It was all work and no sex."

"That's life."

"Tanya was supposed to spend yesterday afternoon with a Realtor she met at a Pilates class to look for a new place to live."

"I talked to the movie's unit production manager," Duncan said. "Jared worked on the set in Lancaster until Wednesday evening. The whole crew can vouch for him. They even took a group selfie with Kevin Costner when the day wrapped. That doesn't mean Jared didn't come back home last night."

"He's got that covered, too. He says there's a woman who can vouch that he was with her in a hotel room all night . . . and he has this." Eve handed Duncan the receipt.

Duncan looked at it and handed it back to Eve. "I'm surprised he didn't have a signed deposition from the woman to go along with the Costner selfie and the hotel receipt."

"What about his truck?"

"CSU says the truck appears clean. By that I mean, they didn't find blood or anything unusual in their cursory check. They took some dirt and fiber samples for analysis just to be safe. But the fucking gentleman is still at the top of my suspect list."

"Because he's the only name on it so far."

"He's got a strong motive," Duncan said.

"But no opportunity," Eve said.

"He wanted them out of his life. He could have hired somebody to do the job."

That was true, but she didn't buy it. "Did you reach Tanya's ex-husband?"

"Merced PD went by his place. He was distraught to hear that his kids were missing. He hasn't left Merced in weeks and his employer can vouch for him being at work the last two days," he said. "There's even video from security cameras at his office and at his home to prove it. They gave me links to see the footage online."

"Has there been any activity on Tanya's cell phone or credit cards?"

"Nope," Duncan said.

"So we're back where we started," Eve said, "with a missing family and a house covered with blood."

"If I were you, I'd write up your notes for the case file, then go back to the house for another walk-through of the crime scene. Maybe CSU will have a clearer picture of what happened."

"What will you be doing?"

"Practicing for my retirement by eating dinner with the wife and binge-watching *Downton Abbey*."

Eve returned to the interrogation room, and Jared gave her the slip of paper. There was very little written on it. He listed only two female friends, one of them Alexis, and the names of the hairdresser, nail salon, Pilates studio, and acting class that she frequented. Either Tanya didn't have much of a social life or, if she did, Jared didn't care about it.

"Thanks for this," she said. "We'll have a deputy take you back to your truck, but you'll have to find another place to stay."

"For how long?"

"A few days," she said.

He thought about that for a moment. "Will you

be reimbursing me if I can't find a friend to crash with and have to go to a hotel?"

"Why would we do that?"

"Because you're the ones not allowing me to go home."

"There's blood everywhere and it's a possible crime scene," she said. "We're processing the evidence. Would you really want to spend the night there even if we'd let you?"

"What about my clothes? Can I go in and get some stuff?"

"I'm sorry, we can't allow you to remove anything from the house right now," she said.

"So I'm going to be out of pocket on clothes, too."

"I guess so," she said.

He shook his head and stood up. "This is fucked."

She asked for his cell phone number, gave him her card, and told him to let her know where he could be reached when he decided where he'd be staying.

Once he was gone, she went to her cubicle and sat down to write up everything that had happened that day and fill out the necessary reports. The Aleve had kicked in by then and so did her hunger. She'd skipped lunch and hadn't had anything to drink in hours. Eve ordered a small pizza and a Coke from Domino's, had it delivered to the front desk, and worked through dinner at her cubicle, managing to get grease on her blouse to go with the dirt. It was after 9:00 p.m. when she finished her paperwork and headed back out to Topanga in a plain-wrap Explorer.

The house and the grounds were lit up by portable floodlights so crime scene techs could see where they were going and so deputies could spot any interlopers. One of the benefits of being deep in Topanga was that there were very few neighbors or other onlookers for the deputies to keep away. But that would change soon. Eve saw two TV satellite trucks setting up down the street for live broadcasts on the late local news. Once the details got out, the number of reporters and lookie-loos would increase exponentially.

She put on rubber gloves and Tyvek shoe covers in her car and entered the house through the kitchen. This was her third time in the crime scene and each visit provoked a different reaction. The first time she'd felt the urgency of the mission and the shock of what she'd discovered. The second time, her reaction was emotional. Now she found herself feeling detached, her interest more clinical and detail oriented. It may also have been a reaction to how the house and circumstances had changed.

There were now multicolored plastic cones on the floor and numbered pieces of tape on the walls to mark different kinds of evidence.

A lot more technicians were in the house, collecting samples, taking photos, and making measurements, creating a work environment alive with activity and purpose. It was a stage that had been reset for the second act.

Eve went to the refrigerator and examined a child's crayon drawing of a dog, presumably Jack Shit, pinned to the appliance with a plunger-shaped magnet from Mr. Plunger. It wasn't the emotional tug of the artwork that drew her interest. It was spots of blood on the paper that were at eye level to her. The spots got larger as Eve followed the spray over the cupboards and down across the boxes of cereal and granola bars on the counter.

Nan Baker came into the kitchen and Eve turned to her. The CSU chief had a surgical mask over her nose and mouth.

"Can you tell me what happened?" Eve asked.

Nan lowered her face mask to speak. "I can say with reasonable certainty that three people and a dog were stabbed to death and dismembered in this house."

# CHAPTER EIGHT

Eve wasn't surprised by Nan's conclusion but it confirmed her worst fears about what she was dealing with. "How can you be so sure?"

"There are three groups of bloodstain patterns in three separate areas of the house, three places where there's significant blood saturation, and three places where there are drag patterns of blood on the carpets and floors that lead to the bathroom. That tells me that three people were assaulted, fell, bled extensively for a while, and then were dragged into the bathroom, where we've found bone, brain matter, and other fragments consistent with dismemberment."

"How do you know it's human blood?"

Nan gave her a withering look that immediately made Eve regret asking the question. But Eve was just trying to cover every base.

"It was obvious to me it was blood and from the amount and the spatter that it was human. But even so, we first test stains we think are blood with tetramethylbenzidine, to determine if we are correct, and then do a field test using HemDirect to determine if it's animal or human. As it turns out, we did find a small amount of animal blood, but I will get into that shortly."

*That would be the dog.* Eve asked, "When did the attacks happen?"

"Timing bloodstains is very tricky and depends on many environmental factors, so the best I can give you at this point is an educated guess, based on the weather and how dry the blood is in various places in the house," Nan said. "I'd say sometime Wednesday morning or afternoon. It's hard to be certain without the bodies."

"How many assailants were there?"

"The evidence at this time indicates only one. That's based primarily on footprints in the blood. Unless the assailant or assailants were capable of levitation, it would have been impossible to walk through this kind of carnage without leaving footprints of some kind, even if their shoes were covered with booties."

Eve noted how carefully Nan qualified her conclusions to cover her ass in case she overlooked something or new information came to light. "Are there any signs of forced entry?"

"Not that we can see," Nan said.

The CSU chief was covering her ass again. But her preliminary conclusion suggested to Eve that the assailant came in through an unlocked door or window or had a key.

"I can only speculate on the sequence of events," Nan said. "But based on the law of superposition—"

Eve interrupted. "Layers of artifacts will be deposited by age, with the oldest at the bottom."

Nan was clearly irritated by the interruption. But Eve was only trying to show the CSU chief that it wasn't necessary to spoon-feed things to an apparently neophyte detective. Eve knew more than people thought.

"Yes, that's right," Nan said, "and it gives us a starting point. Unfortunately, the killer removed evidence, starting with the bodies themselves. He also attempted to clean up some of his work, particularly in the bathroom, with cleansers. But there was just too much blood. So he tried to taint what was left behind with bleach and motor oil, a trick I'm assuming he picked up from all those damn *CSI* shows on television."

That explained the odd smell and why it conjured images in Eve's mind of an over-chlorinated pool and an auto mechanic.

"But we can still tell quite a lot by looking at the bloodstain patterns," Nan continued. "The first attack happened here in the kitchen."

Eve knew that. The blood was a storyboard, every bit as vivid as comic book panels in describing the action that occurred. That's because, as Eve learned in her training and through her own reading, there were many different kinds of bloodstains, and each indicated the action that caused the blood to be spilled, including impact or projected stains, passive stains, and transfer stains. A spatter stain, for example, was the result of an external force hitting liquid blood, while a projection spatter was the result of blood propelled by arterial spray or cast off by an object that struck the liquid blood. A saturation stain will reveal where a victim fell and bled extensively. Eve could see right away what happened in the kitchen and said so.

"Tanya was the victim, judging by the height of the projection spatter and the purse on the floor. She came back from her nine a.m. Pilates class and wanted something to eat. That's when she was confronted by an intruder, who slashed her across the throat, and she fell here." Eve tapped her foot near the puddle of blood. "But she didn't bleed out here or there would be a lot more blood."

Eve looked up to see Nan glaring at her with her arms crossed under her chest.

"You can stop trying to impress me, Detective. I don't care how you got into Homicide or if you're qualified to be there. My job is only to give you the facts as I see them. Do you want to hear them or would you prefer to continue with your own analysis? Because I have lots of work I can be doing."

Eve felt her face flush with embarrassment. She wasn't trying to impress Nan, at least not intentionally—she was just thinking out loud.

"I'm sorry. Go ahead. Please."

Nan uncrossed her arms, acknowledging the apology with a nod, and went on. "Your analysis is essentially correct. The blood trail indicates the killer dragged Tanya out of here, down the hall, and into the master bedroom."

The CSU chief led Eve into the master bedroom and stopped at the foot of the bed. "He lifted her onto the bed and stabbed her repeatedly in a wild rage."

"What makes you think he was angry?"

"The amount of spatter on the walls, headboard, and nightstand suggest a rapid, powerful succession of blows, more like hacking than stabs. Some wounds were so deep that the knife went through her into the mattress." Nan pointed to the deep rips and tears in the blood-soaked mattress.

"She was butchered," Eve said.

"Yes, she was, but not here. She was yanked off the bed and dragged out of the bedroom"—Nan abruptly marched out and Eve followed her to the bathroom door—"and into the bathtub, where she was dismembered."

"With what?"

"Probably the same knife that was used to kill her."

"How do you know it was that knife and not something else?"

"Something like a hacksaw or an ax would

have left bone and tissue fragments distinctively different from what we've found."

"He knew what he was doing," Eve said.

Nan shook her head. "I wouldn't say that. Anyone who has carved a turkey knows how to cut at the joints. But it's hard, messy work dismembering a body. It would have taken him a couple of hours, not counting the time spent on the dog."

"Where was the dog killed?"

"In the tub, based on the spatter and fur on the tile. But I can't say whether the dog was killed before or after Tanya."

"Do you know if the knife came from the house?"

"My guess is that he brought it with him. The cutlery set in the kitchen is complete and it seems to me that the weapon the killer most likely used is something closer to a tactical hunting knife. That said, I suppose it's possible that someone in the house might have owned a knife like that and could tell you if it's missing."

"The killer was in here a long time," Eve said. "Any chance he left fingerprints, hair, or DNA behind?"

"We're dusting every surface but we're not optimistic. Preliminary indications are that he didn't leave any fingerprints, which tells me he wore gloves. My guess is dish gloves."

"Why dish gloves?"

"Because there's an empty box of them under the sink and no dish gloves anywhere in the house. He also wiped everything down with household cleansers and bleach that we believe he found here in the house." Nan gestured to the one-gallon jugs of Clorox and Simple Green. "There are more bottles of the same brands in the hall closet."

"She bought stuff in bulk to save money." Just like Eve's mom did. Everything they had came from Costco. Eve still did most of her shopping there, not so much to save money but to save time. Buying in bulk meant fewer trips to the grocery store.

"Same goes for the dish gloves, garbage bags, and sponges," Nan said. "We found the empty packaging and wrappers for the bags and sponges under the kitchen sink, too."

Eve noticed what looked like a shoe tread in the blood on the bathroom floor. She hadn't seen it before. "Is that a partial shoe print?"

"A man's work boot is my guess. He tried to wipe the print away but we brought it back with a spritz of Leuco Crystal Violet, which reacts to hemoglobin," Nan said. "It's our secret weapon. We raised more partial shoe impressions throughout the house and in the garage. All the prints and impressions were mixed with blood, cleaners, and motor oil, which tells us they were made after the killings."

"You've told me about Tanya and the dog," Eve said, and then asked the question she was dreading. "What about the kids?"

"He got them at the front door." Nan led Eve out to the entry hall and the two backpacks. "I believe they came home from school and were taking off their backpacks when the killer confronted them. He stabbed the boy first, probably in the throat based on the blood spray, and the girl ran to her room. The killer chased her, leaving the boy to bleed out here."

Nan gestured to a saturation stain in the carpet that proved her point and then walked silently with Eve to Caitlin's room. They stood in the center of the room for a moment. Eve looked at the bed. It was unmade and the pillowcase was missing. Her gaze drifted over the blood spatter on the walls, the stuffed animals, and the Barbie dolls and realized something was wrong.

"The spatter pattern is almost my height," Eve said. "Caitlin wasn't that tall."

"That puzzled me, too. I believe she jumped on her bed and was going for the window when he got her. He grabbed her by the neck or arm with one hand, lifted her up with his other hand, then finished her off on the floor, where she bled out." She gestured with her foot at the big saturation stain on the carpet and the bloody drag marks leading to the door. "Then he dragged both of the bodies to the bathtub and cut them up. He put the body parts in trash bags from the kitchen and carried them out to the garage. And that's where we may have caught a break."

"A big one?"

"Barely visible to the naked eye," Nan said and walked down the hall, stopping near the door to the garage. She squatted and pointed to a single tiny spot of blood on the wall. "This spot of blood is unique. It's fresh, nondiluted, and it's nowhere near where the killings occurred."

"So it fell after the killings," Eve said.

"And only one person walked out of here alive," Nan said. "He might have cut himself struggling with a victim or while dismembering a body. We'll run the blood for DNA, but don't get too excited. If he, a parent, or sibling aren't already in the system, it won't tell you who he is."

"But it might convict him once he's caught," Eve said. Then a smear of blood on the floor caught her eye. It was similar to the shoe print in the bathroom but it was smaller and with a different pattern. "What's that?"

"Another shoe print, made in the blood and motor oil that was used to dilute the evidence," she said. "The shoe belongs to one of the children, so we know it was created after the killings."

"How is that footprint possible?"

"The shoe probably fell out of an overstuffed

trash bag that he was carrying," Nan said. "It underscores that he took all the evidence that he could with him—soiled bedding, gloves, clothes, and the bodies, of course. I'm sure he would have pulled up the soiled carpeting and taken it, too, if he could."

"It would have been easier to set fire to the house."

"Maybe he didn't want to draw a crowd here too soon," Nan said. "But that's your department. I'm not a detective."

The killer had been in this house for hours, killing, dismembering, and cleaning up after himself. This was not a man in a hurry. Eve wondered why he wasn't worried that Jared or somebody else might show up. Or would he have just butchered them, too? Had he been watching the house and keeping track of Jared's work schedule? Or, as Duncan suggested, had the killer been hired by Jared and known that nobody would be coming home?

Nan opened the door to the garage and they went inside. There was a washer and dryer against the wall to their left and a metal shelving unit full of gallon jugs of Kirkland detergent and bulk packages of paper towels and toilet paper. The floor was painted concrete with swirls of blood on top created when the killer tried to mop up the mess. Amid the swirls, a couple of footprints stood out.

"It looks like he tried to mop up his footprints," Eve said and gestured to a mop and bucket against the far wall beside a Walmart bag, which she could see contained more cleaning supplies and trash bags.

"He did a pretty good job of it, too," Nan said. "But we were able to raise them anyway."

Eve walked to the end of the blood trail, where there were old stains, infused with dirt and leaves, from fluids that had leaked from a car over a long period of time. She wondered if the car was the Taurus parked in the driveway. "Did you find anything in Tanya's car?"

"No, it was clean. Not a spec of the blood, cleansers, or motor oil that we found in the house."

"Did he already have a car stowed in the garage when Tanya came home or did he bring it over later to haul away everything?"

"I have no idea," Nan said. "That's a mystery you'll have to solve on your own."

Eve spent a few more minutes walking through the crime scene, taking lots of pictures with her phone, hoping something would stick out and reveal some answers to her, but nothing did.

She walked out of the house and spotted reporter Kate Darrow and her cameraman waiting at the plain-wrap Explorer. Darrow was a familiar face on local news who wanted to be taken seriously as a journalist but had sabotaged herself by getting a boob job and dressing to accentuate her sex appeal. It was a shame, Eve thought, because Darrow was tenacious and smart and didn't kiss anybody's ass.

Darrow was widely disliked within the sheriff's department. She'd interviewed the tearful families of the gang members who were beaten by sheriff's deputies at the county jail. There was no excuse for the beatings, but Eve and most of the rank and file within the department were infuriated by Darrow depicting the victims—imprisoned for crimes ranging from rape to murder—as sweet, innocent little angels.

The scandal seemed to deepen with each passing day as new revelations emerged. A half dozen deputies were charged by the FBI with beating prisoners or staging fights among them and gambling on the outcome. Other deputies were charged with smuggling in cell phones and drugs to prisoners. And still other deputies and supervisors were charged with covering up the various crimes.

The latest revelation was that three of the deputies accused of beating prisoners had matching badge-and-skull tattoos hidden under their sleeves that suggested they were members of a secret, perhaps racist society within the department.

Given Darrow's history covering the depart-ment, Eve knew that talking to her was taking a big risk. If Eve said the wrong thing, there could be massive blowback. But there was no way she could get to her car and avoid the reporter. So Eve went to the CSU truck, stripped off her gloves and booties and dropped them in the disposal bag, then approached Darrow like a woman on a mission.

The cameraman swung his camera her way and illuminated her with the spotlight on top. Darrow thrust a microphone in Eve's face. The local news was at 11:00, and it was 10:15 p.m., so at least they weren't live. That took some of the pressure off Eve.

"Detective Ronin, what can you tell me about the bloodbath in there?"

It was a question packed with land mines. "If you want a comment, you'll rephrase the question."

Darrow forced a smile and took a different approach. "We've heard from various sources that an extremely violent crime occurred in that house and that the family who lives there is missing. Is it an abduction or something worse?"

That was a fair question. "For now, all I can say is that Tanya Kenworth and her two children, Caitlin and Troy, are missing. We'd like anyone who has seen or had contact with them in the last forty-eight hours to call our toll-free tip line."

"Do you believe they have been seriously injured?"

Eve ignored the question, got into her car, and drove off. Not that evading the question made any difference. Eve was certain that Darrow already knew the answers to all the questions that she'd asked . . . and so would everybody who would be watching.

And Darrow knew that, too.

# CHAPTER NINE

Eve went back to the empty squad room and laid out what she knew about the crime across several dry-erase boards. She started by creating a timeline, adding the information they had to it and illustrating the facts with printouts of her crime scene photos, a headshot of Tanya's that Eve downloaded from the extra's casting agency, and pictures of Caitlin and Troy that Duncan got from their school.

Her phone vibrated in her pocket. She took it out and saw MOM on the caller ID. Eve surprised herself by answering the call. "Hey, Mom, I'm kind of busy right now."

"I just saw you on the news," Jen said. She had a scratchy voice that men found sexy but that Eve knew came from cigarettes and alcohol. Eve could swear that she smelled the cigarettes through the phone. "Kate Darrow is a knockout. She looks like an actress playing a reporter."

"It's the boobs," Eve said, feeling her shoulder muscles becoming rebar.

"At least she knows how to use hers."

"I'm a cop, Mom. It wouldn't be appropriate for me to dress like that unless I was going undercover as an escort."

"You looked like a hobo next to her. You don't

appreciate how lucky you are to be getting so much screen time."

"I don't want it." Eve knew it infuriated her mother to hear her throwing away something that Jen always wanted and considered priceless.

"The camera loves her and it could love you, too, if you made an effort. It takes two seconds to put on lip gloss and you can do wonders with concealer."

"I don't carry makeup with me on the job."

"Would it have killed you to take off the hat?"

"I really don't have time for this, Mom. You saw the news. I'm in the middle of a homicide investigation."

"I'm well aware of what you're doing. I was on the FBI's Criminal Behavior Task Force."

"You wore an FBI windbreaker and stood in the background on a *Criminal Minds* episode. It's not the same thing."

"It still haunts me," she said.

Eve saw Deputy Ross walk in with a stack of papers. "I have to go, Mom. Love you. Bye."

Ross dropped the papers on the table beside her. "Here are the reports from the canvas of the neighborhood and a list of license plates from the cars parked at the Topanga Park trailheads."

"Anything come up?" She rolled her shoulders, trying to loosen the rigid muscles.

"I spoke to a woman who says her son rode home on the school bus yesterday with Caitlin and

Troy," Ross said. "When they got to their stop on Entrada, the kid saw them walking home like they always do. That would've been about two fifteen."

"Thanks, that's very helpful." Eve was tempted to ask him for a shoulder rub or maybe something more. She'd noticed his strong hands and warm smile. Those could melt the rebar but that wasn't a real option.

The deputy walked out and Eve added the information about the kids to the timeline. She picked up the stack of reports and took them to her cubicle so she could go through them. That's when Captain Moffett came in.

"I saw you on the news," he said. "I'm not happy about it."

"I couldn't avoid Darrow and I thought a 'no comment' answer to her question would confirm what she said about a bloodbath and they'd run with that."

"You made the right call."

"So what's the problem?"

"Look at yourself, Ronin. Your jacket and pants are filthy, there's a stain on your blouse, and that baseball cap makes you look like a teenager. It reflects badly on the department."

She was tempted to ask if her mother had called him, too, but instead she said: "I'm sorry, sir."

"Go home, take a shower, get some sleep, and come back tomorrow in a clean set of clothes. Maybe keep a spare set in your locker."

"Yes, sir."

The captain headed for the door, then paused before walking out. "I've ordered a search party with dogs to start going through the woods around the house tomorrow morning."

"What changed your mind?"

"You just told the world that the family was slaughtered and we have nothing to go on."

"That's not what I said."

"That's what everybody heard and what we all know is true. The sooner we find the corpses, the faster we'll find the killer."

He continued out the door. She stood there for a moment, thinking about what the captain said, and about why she was wearing the baseball cap. She'd forgotten it was still there and realized now that taking it off was going to be a painful problem. It was stuck to her hair with blood.

She took out her phone and texted her sister, Lisa, who was an ER nurse at West Hills Hospital, which was about six miles north of Calabasas.

> Could you drop by my place when your shift is over? Bring your first aid kit.

She left the building by the rear exit, where her ten-speed bike was parked, along with all the squad cars, the mobile command center, the helicopter, and everybody's personal vehicles.

Eve put on her helmet carefully over her

baseball cap, got on her bike, and rode off, heading east on Agoura Road. She crossed Lost Hills Road and continued on toward Las Virgenes Road, better known by the locals as Malibu Canyon. Along the way, she passed by a shopping center, the Good Nite Inn, and several office buildings, none taller than three stories so nothing would obscure the views of the open hills to the north and east.

When Eve reached Las Virgenes, she turned left and cycled across the 101 freeway overpass to the residential area on the other side. There were undeveloped hills to her left and three townhouse condominium complexes to her right. She lived in a two-story unit on the street. Her windows faced the charred hills and blackened oaks that burned a year ago in a wildfire that started thirty miles north in Stevenson Ranch and was blown west by the hot Santa Ana winds before being put out at the freeway.

She got off her bike at the curb, wheeled it to the front door, and brought it inside, parking it in her entry hall at the base of the stairs. Her living room walls were bare and the dinette set, coffee table, couch, and entertainment center all came from IKEA.

Eve went upstairs to her bedroom and stripped out of her clothes, but she kept on her cap. The dried blood in her hair had stuck to it and she didn't want to pull any hair out. She got into the shower, stuck her head under the hot water, then eased the wet cap off her head, only losing a few hairs in the process.

The water was scalding, just how she liked it, but the water flow was weak, part of the state's efforts to conserve water during what was becoming a permanent drought. She shampooed her hair and saw the red swirling amid the white foam at her feet. It brought back unsettling images of Tanya's bloody bathroom.

She stepped out of the shower and dried off, looking at her reflection in the full-length mirror on the bathroom door. The bruise on her flat stomach was a deep, angry purple. She pressed her ribs, took some deep breaths, and feeling no sharp pains, satisfied herself that nothing was broken. She got out some cotton swabs and rubbing alcohol and gently cleaned the wound on her head.

Eve slipped on a tank top and sweats and went downstairs, where her sister was standing at the kitchen counter, still in her blue nursing scrubs, eating chocolate ice cream out of a container. This was not the first time Lisa had let herself into Eve's place.

Lisa and Eve shared their mother's piercing blue eyes but not much else, thanks to having different fathers. Lisa was shorter, rounder, though not chubby, and had curly black hair.

"You look better than you did on TV tonight," Lisa said.

Now it was official. Everybody thought she looked terrible. "How did you see it at work?"

Lisa handed the spoon to Eve, who carved out a chunk of chocolate ice cream for herself. "It was on in the waiting room. They said a single mother and her two little kids disappeared and that there's blood all over the house."

"I wish that stuff about the crime scene hadn't come out yet." Eve gave Lisa the spoon and her sister took another bite. They continued sharing the spoon back-and-forth as they talked. "But I suppose it could be worse."

"It could?"

"Much worse. You don't want to know."

"They also mentioned that the mother was an aspiring actress."

"Isn't everybody in LA?" Eve asked.

"Tell me she doesn't remind you of Mom and that you aren't seeing me and Kenny in those missing kids."

"I haven't had a chance to think about the similarities."

That was a lie. The parallels were striking and she couldn't help but see her herself in Caitlin, which made the gruesome murders even more horrible to contemplate.

"But you're feeling them," Lisa said, "which is why you asked me to make a house call."

Lisa was always attuned to the emotions at play in a situation, which is why she got hurt so easily by tension in the house when they were growing up. It was also why Eve had felt such a strong need to minimize the strife around them any way she could. But it was a futile effort. Eve was undermined by her mom's irrational behavior at every turn.

"Actually, what I'm feeling is a headache and, thanks to the ER stories you've told me, I'm worried about the risk of a subdural hematoma."

"Were you hit on the head today?"

"Yes," Eve said. "With a rock."

"How hard?"

"I might have passed out for a minute or two."

"Damn it." Lisa took the spoon and the ice cream away from Eve. "Sit down."

Eve took a seat at the kitchen table. Lisa rummaged angrily in her purse, took out a penlight, and shined it into Eve's eyes.

"Why didn't you go to the hospital?" Lisa asked.

"There was too much happening with the investigation," she said. "But I did ask an ER nurse to come to my house with a first aid kit."

"When you say that, it usually means ice cream and a sympathetic ear, not medical supplies," Lisa said. "Look right and then left without moving your head."

Eve did as she was told. Lisa put down the penlight and held a finger up in front of Eve's face.

"Now follow my finger." Lisa moved her finger

from left to right, then up and down. "What day is it?"

"Thursday."

Lisa lowered her finger. "What was the name of the director Mom dated with the '70s porn star mustache?"

"Hank Bloom."

"How many times has Mom had a boob job?"

"Three," Eve said. "Why are you asking me all these questions?"

"I'm checking your mental acuity." Lisa examined the wound on Eve's head. "It doesn't look like you need any stitches. When was your last tetanus shot?"

"Two years ago when I got that dog bite."

"I think you'll live," Lisa said. "What about the woman and kids you're looking for?"

"They're dead," Eve said. "We just haven't found their bodies yet."

Lisa gave her sister a long, appraising look. "Don't make this case personal, Eve, though it's laughable for me to say that."

"What's that supposed to mean?" Eve picked up the spoon and started working on the ice cream again.

"You don't have to be Dr. Phil to know why you became a cop. You've been trying to impose order on Mom and the world and take care of everybody since you were born. This case is going to play you."

"Dr. Phil is an asshole," Eve said. "His name, and the fact that he is on TV, should tell you all you need to know. What real doctor would drop his last name and analyze patients in front of a studio audience? Only an asshole."

"I think you're missing the point," Lisa said. "Or purposely avoiding it."

"Why did you become a nurse?"

"Probably the same reason you became a cop—to make up for something I was missing in my life. Someone to take care of me."

"I took care of you," she said.

"I was also emulating a terrific role model. People are complicated."

"Not according to Dr. Phil."

Lisa gave Eve a hug. "I'm going home to bed. You should get some sleep now, too."

"I can spare three hours for a quick nap."

"You just said the family is dead."

Eve sighed. "But the killer isn't."

# CHAPTER TEN

Lisa was barely out the door when Eve changed her mind about the nap. Sleeping wouldn't move the case forward. All the talking about her mom made Eve think about family. It nagged at her that she hadn't spoken face-to-face with Cleve Kenworth, Tanya's ex-husband and the father of the kids. He was the closest relative to those dead kids. The Merced Police had talked to him but she hadn't looked him in the eye. She decided it would be an investigative mistake if she didn't meet with him as soon as possible.

Merced was 273 miles north of Calabasas in California's Central Valley, a straight shot up Interstate 5 and Highway 99 and there would be almost no traffic at this time of night. If she drove at ninety miles an hour, it would take her three hours to get there. That was a much better use of her time than sleep.

So she got dressed, rode her bike to the Lost Hills station, checked out a plain-wrap Explorer, and headed for Merced. She lit up the flashers behind the front grille and put the magnetized swirling bubble light up on the roof so everybody, particularly any California Highway Patrol cars hiding in speed traps, would see her coming.

Eve slowed only to go down the Grapevine, the

winding route out of the Tehachapi Mountains into the southern-most end of the San Joaquin Valley, because it was dangerous even at normal speeds and there was a big CHP weigh station at the bottom. Racing past the CHP station, unless she was in hot pursuit of a felon, would have been obnoxious and just asking for trouble.

Once she hit the valley, the freeway split off into a continuation of Interstate 5, heading up the sparsely populated western edge, and the older Highway 99, which went straight up the center and hit all the major agricultural communities, from Bakersfield to Sacramento. Eve took the 99, a journey through vast expanses of pitch-black farmland where half of the nation's fruits, vegetables, and nuts were grown. *At least for now,* she thought. After years of drought, the underground aquifers were being sucked dry and the crops were baking. Soon, the valley could be a dust bowl.

To stay awake, she cranked up the AC to keep herself uncomfortably chilled and listened to one of Michael Connelly's Harry Bosch crime novels. Bosch was an LAPD detective who, over a thirty-year career that spanned about as many books, solved one major murder after another and yet his bosses still doubted his skill and integrity, regularly undermined his work, and repeatedly investigated him for misconduct. It frustrated her even more than it did him. His problem, she thought, was that he didn't know how to play politics. She'd already proven that she could. Now she had to prove she could do the job.

Eve arrived in Merced at 4:30 a.m. She drove up G Street, past the unoccupied storefronts downtown, under the railroad tracks, and across the dry creek to the bedroom side of town. The shopping centers and homes became more suburban looking the closer she got to the new University of California campus.

Cleve's neighborhood was full of recently built Spanish-Mediterranean tract houses with FOR SALE and FOR RENT signs in their dead lawns. His home was one of the few without a sign and had an old Chevy Malibu in the driveway. She parked in front of Cleve's dark house, shut off her engine, and closed her eyes for a moment.

Eve was awakened by someone rapping a knuckle on the driver's side window. The sun was up, though only barely, and a white guy in a bathrobe and pajamas was standing beside her car, a newspaper tucked under his arm. He was in his thirties, about six feet tall with a paunch, and had dark circles under bloodshot eyes. She rolled down the window.

"Yes?" she said. "Can I help you?"

"I was just wondering why a police officer is parked in front of my house at six in the morning," he said.

"How do you know I'm a police officer?" she

91

asked. The man took the bubble light off the top of her car and handed it to her. She forgot she'd left it up there. "Are you Cleve Kenworth?"

"Yeah," he said.

"I'm Detective Eve Ronin from the Los Angeles County Sheriff's Department. I'd like to talk with you."

"You drove all the way up here last night?" he asked.

She nodded. "I got in about an hour or so ago."

"You should have knocked on the door when you got here."

"I didn't want to wake you."

"I haven't been able to sleep. I just sat in the recliner all night, thinking about where Caty and Troy might be." He wiped a tear from his eye. Now she knew why they were so bloodshot.

"Can I come in?"

He looked back at the house, then at her. "My girlfriend and her kids are up now. Tell you what. I'll meet you at Paul's Place in ten minutes. It's a coffee shop on G Street."

"I'll find it," she said.

She watched Cleve, his shoulders slouched, shuffle back into the house. He was carrying a lot of sadness and she knew he'd soon be carrying a lot more.

# CHAPTER ELEVEN

Paul's was a lot like the coffee shops that used to be all over Los Angeles, like Ships, Bob's Big Boy, and Sambo's, but were fast becoming extinct. Eve loved them and this one was the real deal. The tabletops in each vinyl-upholstered booth were shellacked with business cards from local merchants, something she'd never seen before. The place was popular. There were at least two dozen customers at this early hour.

She ordered coffee from a young waitress who looked like a college student squeezing in a job before her day of classes. Cleve showed up a few minutes later and ordered a cup of coffee, too. He wore jeans and a UC Merced sweatshirt. GO BOBCATS! was written across the chest.

"Have you been to Merced before?" he asked.

"Not really. I took a prisoner to Atwater Penitentiary once and stopped at the In-N-Out off the freeway here on my way back to LA."

"I was born and raised here. Half the population is Hispanic, another twelve percent is Asian, mostly Hmong refugees. We've got a twelve percent unemployment rate and twenty-eight percent of our adult population didn't graduate high school. Home values have dropped sixty percent from ten years ago. Sixty percent. I keep asking myself why I stay."

"There must be something that keeps you from moving."

"Family, I suppose. My heart is here, well, half of it, anyway. The other half is in LA with my kids." Cleve looked into his empty coffee cup. "The Merced cops came by the office yesterday. All they told me is that Tanya and the kids are gone and there might be 'foul play' involved. What does that even mean? I've been imagining the worst. I can't help it. I need to know if my kids are okay. Are they okay?"

She didn't want to tell him yet that they were dead and dismembered. She was spared giving him an immediate evasive answer by the waitress, who filled Cleve's coffee cup and refilled Eve's. Once the waitress was gone, Eve spoke in a low voice.

"A friend of Tanya's reported her missing yesterday and your kids didn't show up for school. We went to the house to investigate and discovered evidence of a struggle. Now we're searching for Tanya and your kids. I'm hoping you can help us find them by answering a few questions."

"You aren't telling me everything."

"No, I'm not."

"Because you think I had something to do with whatever has happened to them."

"I need to rule that out," she said.

"What about Tanya's boyfriend?"

"What about him?"

"He's beating my kids and I wouldn't be surprised if he's abusing her, too." Cleve poured four sugars into the coffee and took a sip. It seemed to take some of the grogginess from his face. "I told her to get the hell out of there or I'd go to court for custody of the kids. She said I was overreacting to a little 'parental discipline' but he isn't the Goddamn parent in that house—she is."

Eve took out her pad and pen and began making notes. "What kind of discipline are we talking about?"

"Troy told me that Jared slapped him across the face for drinking out of a carton of milk. Knocked the carton right out of his hands and got milk all over him. Caty saw the whole thing. And gave him hell. She's very protective of her brother. She treats him more like her child."

Eve had felt the same way about her brother and sister when she was growing up. She still did.

"Where was Tanya?" Eve asked.

Cleve scowled. "She was off 'acting' somewhere when it happened. She thinks she's a star. That's why we split."

She thought about Caitlin, caught between her mom and her dad and Jared, just trying to hold everything together, to create some kind of stability for herself and her brother separate from the shit happening around them. She knew exactly how Caitlin felt. In fact, just thinking about it brought back that same anxious pressure in her chest again, as if she were still trapped in that situation herself.

"Tell me more about why you broke up." It probably wasn't relevant but she wanted to keep him talking about the family dynamics and see if something useful to her came out.

"We'd been married about four years." He took another sip of coffee, to fortify himself. "I was long-haul trucking because there was no work here. She was a housewife and doing plays at the community theater. The newspaper called her the 'Meryl Streep of Merced.' The talent pool isn't very deep here. Before Tanya came along, a tree stump was the Meryl Streep of Merced. But it went to her head and she hated it here, not that I can blame her for that. So she took off for LA with the kids. I couldn't fight her for custody back then. But I can now and I told her I would. That's why she dumped Jared . . . which isn't very Goddamn effective if you haven't left his house, is it?"

Her question had paid off in interesting ways. His take on Tanya's breakup contradicted Jared's story. The truth was probably somewhere in between. It was too soon to tell if the difference was significant or not. She was more interested now in Cleve's child custody battle with Tanya.

"What makes you think you can get custody of the kids now?"

"I've got a job that keeps me in town, I'm engaged, and Tanya's an absentee parent with an abusive boyfriend who smacks my kids."

"Did Tanya ever confirm any of the abuse?"

Cleve looked at Eve like she was a moron. "And give me ammo for the judge? Hell no. But the kids will. They hate Jared and love Emily."

"Who is Emily?"

"My fiancée," Cleve said. "We live together. She has two kids from a previous marriage. They are about the same age as Caty and Troy. We'll be a real-life *Brady Bunch*."

"Where were you the last two days?"

The Merced Police covered this but she wanted to hear it for herself.

"Here at work. I sell farming equipment. You can call the office." He leaned forward on the table, narrowing the distance between the two of them, and looked her in the eye. "What you should be asking is where was Jared."

She didn't see the harm in answering that question. "He was on location shooting a Western in Lancaster."

"He's still responsible." Cleve leaned back again. "Maybe she ran off with the kids so Jared couldn't hurt them and I couldn't get custody."

"We're exploring every possibility."

"What are the others?" he asked.

Eve wasn't ready to tell him any of that yet and there was still a lot she didn't know. She glanced at her watch. It could take her longer to get home than it did to get up here. She'd be hitting the city in the middle of the four-hour-long morning "rush hour."

"I need to get back to Los Angeles and the investigation." Eve took out her card and slid it across the table to Cleve. "Here's my contact information. You can call me anytime."

He picked up her card but didn't look at it. "You ask a lot of questions but you don't answer many."

She left a few dollars on the table, slid out of the booth, and stood up. "It's an active investigation, Mr. Kenworth. I don't want to say something now that ends up not being true."

"That's why you won't say if my kids are okay," he said, waiting for her to argue the point, but she didn't. "I'll be in LA by this afternoon. I'll stay there until you find my kids."

"That's not necessary."

"Yes, it is," he said. "I'll call you and let you know where I am when I get there."

# CHAPTER TWELVE

Traffic was heavier on the way back but it didn't make any difference. Drivers saw her flashing lights in the rearview mirror and gave her a wide berth, even in Valencia, where the freeway became a parking lot. The rush-hour drivers came to a dead stop to stare at the columns of smoke coming from a new brush fire in Stevenson Ranch, the flames raging across the parched hills, stoked by low humidity and strong, hot winds from the desert blowing toward the sea. The winds could potentially drive the flames to Malibu, twenty-eight miles away as the crow flies, if they weren't snuffed in a hurry. It had happened before.

Despite the slowdown in Valencia, she managed to get back to the Lost Hills station shortly after 10:00 a.m. Duncan Pavone, Wally Biddle, and Stan Garvey were in the squad room when Eve arrived and were looking at her work on the dry-erase boards. She took a few granola bars from the box in the back and joined them at the boards, letting her eyes drift over the crime scene photos.

"Glad you could make it," Duncan said to her, glancing at his watch. "But I can't blame you for sleeping in. Getting the case up on the board like this must have been a lot of work last night and it's a good thing you did it. Crockett and Tubbs have been assigned to your task force and this has helped me bring them up to speed."

Eve tore open the wrapper on a granola bar and started eating. "When did we become a task force? And when did it become mine?"

"After Sheriff Lansing saw you on the news last night," Duncan said.

"Translation," Biddle said. "You get to run the task force because you're young, you have nice tits, and were in a viral video that got great PR for the department in the middle of the county jail shitstorm."

Garvey added, "As opposed to one of the detectives who've actually spent years grinding away and solving homicides and know what the fuck they're doing."

"Stop whining. This isn't new," she said, getting in his face. "That's the way you've felt since I walked in the door three months ago."

Garvey wasn't intimidated. "What did you expect? A standing ovation from the guys who actually earned their promotions?"

"No, Tubbs, this is exactly what I expected." Eve stepped away from him and shifted her gaze between the three men. "Because it's the same sexist attitude that would have shut me out of Robbery-Homicide for another ten years . . . and that I still would have faced if I ever got in. So I used the leverage that video gave me to get myself here overnight. Did I leapfrog over people who've been struggling to get into Robbery-Homicide for years and haven't made it? Yes, I did. Do I care? Nope. Do I deserve to be here? It doesn't matter because here I am, boys. You don't like it? Too bad. Suck it up or get out. I'm sure the sheriff will give me two other detectives to replace you. They might even stay."

Biddle and Garvey glowered but didn't move. The tension was so thick that it was as palpable as humidity. But it felt great to Eve to finally say what she'd been feeling. She wasn't going to apologize for being ambitious or using the opportunities that came her way to get what she wanted.

She turned her attention back to the crime scene photos and took a bite of her granola bar. *Fuck them.* She had three murders to solve, four if she counted the dog . . . and she did.

Duncan cleared his throat. "Well, now that we've got the housekeeping preliminaries out of the way, let's get to work. You two go talk to Tanya's Pilates instructor and the other women in the class. They were probably the last ones to see her alive and might be able to point us to her Realtor."

Biddle and Garvey headed for the door.

"Wait, before you go," Eve said, her back to them, her eyes still on the board, "there's more you need to know. Tanya's ex-husband, Cleve

Kenworth, claims that her boyfriend, Jared Rawlins, was beating the kids, maybe her, too. So we should probably talk to the teachers at the kids' school, see if they saw any signs of abuse."

Duncan looked at her. "When did you talk to Kenworth?"

"I went up to Merced." Her gaze kept going back to one of the photos from the kitchen and she didn't know why. She gave it a closer look. "That's why I'm late. I just came back."

"You mean, after you did all this," Duncan waved his hand at the board, "you got in a car and drove to Merced."

"I took a shower and changed my clothes first," she said, but her attention was on the photo. It showed the blood spatter on the cupboards and the boxes of food on the counter.

"Did you sleep at all last night?"

"I got a little nap." Eve took a bite of her granola bar, then regarded the empty caramel-colored wrapper in her hand. It was a Nature Valley Sweet & Salty Nut Granola Bar. Her gaze shifted across the squad room to the big box that the bar came from, then to the identical blood-spattered box in the photo of Tanya's kitchen. *Aha, that was it. They both ate the same granola bars. So what?*

Biddle groaned but took his seat again. Garvey leaned against the wall and sighed. Duncan shook his head. Eve looked at the three men, and their judgmental expressions annoyed her.

"What?" Eve said. "I've got a job to do and I'm doing it."

"It isn't laziness or a lack of commitment if you eat, sleep, and occasionally take a crap while you're working a case," Duncan said. "In fact, I do my best thinking on the toilet."

"Is that why you're in there for hours?" Biddle said.

"I got one word for you," Garvey said to Duncan. "Metamucil."

"That's like offering kryptonite to Superman," Duncan said. "I'd never solve a case."

The three men shared a laugh, bonding over her overzealousness, and she let it go because it seemed to dissipate the lingering tension from her speech.

"Cleve thinks Jared is our guy," she said.

"So do I," Duncan said.

"I don't see it," Eve said, her attention shifting back to the damn granola box. It wasn't unusual that Tanya and the detectives bought the same box of granola bars. They were sold in bulk at Costco on an end-cap pallet. Hundreds, if not thousands, of people in the area had the same box in their pantry. So why was it bugging her?

"Here's why I think it's Jared," Duncan said and tapped his finger on one of the crime scene photos of the bathroom. "When there's no sign of a break-in, and there's this kind of bloodshed, the killer is usually someone who had an intimate relationship with the victim and has a lot of rage."

She studied the bathroom photo, paying particular attention to the gallon jugs of Clorox and Simple Green on the sink and the Lysol bottle on the floor.

"That's certainly what we've got here," Biddle said. "This guy is sleeping on the couch in his own fucking house. She might as well have cut off his balls and worn them as a broach. So yeah, Jared looks real good for this. We should be focusing our attention on breaking his way-too-good alibi."

Eve studied the cleansers and realized what was bothering her. There was a string to follow here, but she wasn't sure if it would lead anywhere. She needed to go back to the house to find out.

"Sure, we can do that," Eve said. "Let's get to work."

She headed for the door.

"Where are you going?" Duncan called after her.

"The crime scene," she said. "I want another look."

# CHAPTER THIRTEEN

On the road leading to the cul-de-sac, she passed a Topanga State Park trailhead—a dirt parking lot and a foot trail that led up into the hills. The sheriff's department K-9 unit was using the lot as a staging area and a half dozen deputies and their dogs were preparing to begin their search for Tanya and her kids. *No,* Eve corrected herself, *they were looking for their bodies.*

There were three TV satellite trucks parked at the mouth of the cul-de-sac, the reporters for each station getting ready to broadcast live for the midmorning newscasts, using the crime scene as a backdrop. Eve hoped to blend into the background like an extra and leave before they went on the air.

The CSU van and two patrol cars were parked in front of the house, which was surrounded by crime scene tape and manned by a deputy with a clipboard. She parked in front of the house, put on her gloves and shoe covers, and approached the uniformed deputy who guarded the empty house. It was Clayton, instantly recognizable by his wraparound shades, which there was no reason to be wearing this early in the morning.

He recognized her, too, made a note of her name on his clipboard, and then handed it to her for a signature.

Eve gestured to the news vans as she signed the paper that kept track of everybody who entered the house. "How long have they been here?"

"Since daybreak," Clayton said. "For the morning shows. Otherwise it's been quiet. Only ones in and out have been CSU."

Eve lifted the crime scene tape and went into the kitchen. She peeked into the hallway and saw Noomis cutting a sample from the living room carpet and another tech scraping something off the wall in the hallway. They both nodded at her, acknowledging her presence.

She returned to the kitchen and opened the pantry. There was a 40-ounce jar of Kirkland cashews, a 78-ounce box of Kellogg's Raisin Bran, a box of 3,000 square feet of Kirkland plastic wrap, a 45-pound bag of Kirkland dog food, a box of 48 assorted Nutri-Grain snack bars, and other bulk items, most of them from Kirkland, Costco's own budget brand.

She opened the cupboard under the sink and saw a 135-ounce bottle of Kirkland dish soap, a box of 115 Kirkland Premium Dishwasher Pacs, an empty box of 50 Soft Scrub latex gloves, and a discarded wrapper for 21 Scotch-Brite scrub sponges.

Eve got up and went to the magnet-covered refrigerator, opened it, and looked inside. The items that caught her eye were the 30-ounce container of French's mustard, the box of 25 Stonyfield YoKids Organic Yogurt Squeezers, the 64-ounce jar of Kirkland Signature Real Mayonnaise, the 48-ounce jar of Kirkland Organic Creamy Peanut Butter, and a 48-ounce jar of Smucker's Strawberry Jelly.

She left the kitchen, went down the hall, and paused outside the bathroom door. In addition to the gallon bottles of Clorox and Simple Green on the sink, which were in Eve's crime scene photos, she also saw smaller spray bottles of Clorox and Lysol on the floor. Eve took a picture of them with her phone, then went out to the garage.

Eve walked up to the Walmart bag beside the mop and bucket and crouched beside it to look inside. What was inside gave her a chill. The string had led somewhere.

Eve took several pictures of the Walmart bag and its contents and approached Noomis in the living room.

"Is Nan around?" she asked.

"She's back at the lab," Noomis said. "Is there something I can do for you?"

"There's a Walmart bag on the floor of the garage. I need you to process it as evidence," she said—then another thought occurred to her.

"Are you checking that pee sample on the hill for DNA?"

"Not yet," he said. "The boss didn't think it was a priority."

"It is."

"I'll tell the boss."

"Thanks."

Eve left the house and stopped at the CSU van to remove her gloves and booties and drop them in the disposal bag. While she did that, she warily eyed the three TV reporters, including Darrow, who were waiting for her with their cameramen. There was probably more makeup in Darrow's purse than Eve had bought in the last five years. Eve wasn't wearing anything on her face but a confident expression. At least her clothes were clean. She took a deep breath and went over to meet them with all the enthusiasm of a woman facing a root canal.

"Detective Ronin," Darrow said. "Are there any new developments in the search for Tanya Kenworth and her two children?"

"Nothing that I can share at this time," Eve said.

Another reporter spoke up, an old-timer who had been on TV since Eve was a kid, but she couldn't put a name to his face. "There's a sheriff's department K-9 search team preparing to go into Topanga State Park. Are they looking for bodies?"

"They are looking for any trail that might have been left by Tanya, her kids, or whoever attacked them."

Darrow talked over another reporter who tried to squeeze in a question. "Jared Rawlins, Tanya's boyfriend, told us in an exclusive interview that you described the crime scene as a slaughterhouse. So is this a missing persons case or a homicide investigation?"

Eve didn't say that, Duncan did, and only to get a reaction out of Jared, but it probably wasn't the smartest decision. She wondered what else Jared had told Darrow and if any of it contradicted what he told them.

"We are searching for a family that disappeared under violent circumstances and we are deeply concerned about their safety. That's all I can say right now."

Darrow threw out one more question: "You worked in the county jail. Do you have a badge-and-skull tattoo?"

It was a dumb, provocative question. No woman would ever be invited into a secret society of like-minded deputies. She'd seen a few deputies with the tattoos but had never witnessed a beating, by them or anybody else, during her mandatory time serving at the county jail.

"No, I don't," Eve said.

"What do you think of the deputies who do?"

She hadn't given it any thought and even if she had, she wouldn't share it with the media.

Eve ignored the question, got into her car, and tried to back out without running over any reporters.

# CHAPTER FOURTEEN

Duncan, Biddle, and Garvey were still in the squad room making calls when she returned. She tapped them each on the shoulder and gestured for them to join her at the dry-erase boards when they wrapped up their calls. It only took a minute or two before they all gathered around her. She had news to share, but before she could speak, Biddle began talking.

"I spoke to the kids' teachers at school. Neither kid showed any signs of abuse, physically or emotionally, that the teachers could see. That doesn't mean it wasn't happening, of course. I'm trying to track down their pediatrician to see if I can get their medical records."

"Good work." Eve hadn't called them together to hear their progress. But, once again, she was interrupted before she could share her lead, this time by Garvey.

"Tanya's Pilates instructor is out until this afternoon. I asked for a list of everybody in her class in the meantime but the lady at the front desk won't give me what she has without checking with her supervisor first. But there isn't a regular enrollment, so to speak. People reserve spots online or on a sign-up sheet in the gym until the class fills up. So it can be different people every day. The Realtor may only have shown up once, but I'll keep on it."

"Excellent," Eve said.

Duncan studied Eve's face. "Did something come up at the crime scene?"

"I think so." She took out her phone and held it up to show them a photo of the Walmart bag. The three men crowded around to look at her picture.

"What are we looking at?" Biddle asked.

"A Walmart bag that contains a three-pack of Brillo sponges, a twenty-two-ounce spray bottle of Lysol All-Purpose Cleaner, and an unopened box of forty Glad Strong Quick-Tie thirty-gallon trash bags. There's no receipt inside."

Duncan frowned. "What's unusual about that?"

"It doesn't fit." Eve set down her phone, walked over to the dry-erase board, and pointed to the crime scene photos. "Tanya bought their household staples in bulk at Costco and chose the cheap Kirkland-brand version of anything whenever she had a choice. That's typical for a family on a tight budget trying to stretch every dollar. Most of the empty bottles of cleanser in the bathroom are bulk size, except for these two on the floor and the ones in the Walmart bag that are regular size. Those are the only two bottles of Lysol in the house, by the way."

"So what?" Garvey said.

"Tanya already had plenty of cleansers, sponges, and trash bags," Eve said. "Why would

112

she go to Walmart to buy more, and in regular sizes, when she already had so much?"

Duncan nodded, seeing her point. "You think the killer brought the regular-size bottles of Clorox and Lysol with him but then saw that she had plenty of her own and used those."

"No," she said. "I think he got them afterwards."

"You're saying this guy ran out of cleaning supplies," Duncan said, "so he took a break from dismembering three people and a dog to go shopping at Walmart?"

"He probably disposed of the bodies and cleaned himself up first," she said. "But yes, that's what I'm saying."

Garvey shook his head, not buying it. "Killers don't come and go from bloody crime scenes. It's too risky."

"This one does," she said. "I think he was the guy who jumped me on the hill that overlooks the house."

It made a lot more sense to her than Duncan's theory that she'd disturbed some crazed homeless person, not that she had any evidence to back it up.

Duncan said, "Why would he come back to the house the day after the killings?"

"For his sleeping bag. He didn't want to leave behind any evidence that he'd been watching the house before the murders."

"That's a leap," Duncan said. "We don't know that it wasn't a homeless person's campsite."

"We don't know that it was. There's no evidence either way, but given where the campsite was, and the view it has of the house, my theory gives us a motive why someone was up there and willing to clobber a cop to get away with his stuff."

"If you're right," Biddle said, "and he did all of that coming and going to the crime scene, then this guy must have Godzilla's balls."

"Or he's insane," Garvey said.

"But it confirms Duncan's Doctrine," Biddle said, eliciting a smile from Duncan.

"What is that?" Eve asked.

"Most crimes have a Walmart connection," Duncan said.

"It's like six degrees of separation," Garvey said. "Only with Walmart."

"Almost never fails," Duncan said and went to his cubicle. "That's why I have Walmart's regional supervisor on my speed dial."

# CHAPTER FIFTEEN

Duncan asked Walmart's regional manager to check their local stores for any purchases made on Tuesday and Wednesday that matched the bar codes of the items in the shopping bag at the crime scene. The regional manager came back with a hit at the Walmart at the Fallbrook Center in Canoga Park.

It was a fifteen-minute drive from the Lost Hills station. Eve and Duncan met Bert, a pudgy guy in a blue Walmart vest, in front of the in-store McDonald's. Bert was the store manager.

"We had a customer at 10:47 p.m. on Wednesday night who bought the items on your list," Bert said. "But they were only part of his purchases."

"What else did he buy?" Eve asked.

"A bag of Doritos, a box of Ding Dongs, a six-pack of Coke, and a DVD."

"The guy eats like a ten-year-old," Duncan said. "Did he use a credit card?"

"He paid cash," Bert said.

"Of course he did," Duncan said.

"But we have him on video," Bert said. "I can show you."

"That would be great," Eve said.

Bert led them off the sales floor and into a

tiny windowless room just large enough to hold a console of security monitors and two office chairs with torn upholstery that had been repaired with strips of duct tape.

"I've got it cued up for you," Bert said, settling into a creaking chair and hitting a button on the keyboard.

The screens showed various high angles on a white man in his late twenties or early thirties, in decent physical shape, about six feet tall, with a few days' growth of patchy stubble on his pale, angular face. His short brown hair was wet and messy, like he'd washed it, dried it quickly with a towel, and didn't bother combing or brushing it afterward, which Eve thought was exactly the explanation.

He wore a navy-blue T-shirt and jeans and was rummaging around in a bargain bin that was nearly overflowing with cheap DVDs. His shopping cart contained Doritos, Ding Dongs, the Cokes, as well as two bottles each of Clorox and Lysol cleanser, the box of trash bags, and the sponges. Eve felt an almost electric charge shoot up her spine. This was the killer. She was certain of it.

"He's got everything we found at the crime scene," she said.

"Except for the DVD and snacks," Duncan said. "What was he planning to do? Relax with a movie after he finished cleaning up?"

They watched the man sort through the DVDs, pick one out, and continue on to the cashier at the front of the store.

"What movie did he buy?" Eve asked.

*Planet of the Apes.* The original one with Charlton Heston." Bert twisted his face into a snarl and spoke with a raw, angry voice: "Take your stinking paws off me, you damned dirty ape!"

The reference to the movie scene made Eve think back on the beast that attacked her. Could it have been an ape? It was ridiculous, and she immediately dismissed the thought as the result of her fatigue.

"That last shot of the Statue of Liberty is the best twist ending of all time," Bert added.

"Which you just ruined for me," Duncan said. "Do you have any cameras on the parking lot?"

"Only the area directly in front of the store." Bert hit a few more keys and the monitors showed high angles looking down into the first space or two of the four parking aisles directly in front of the store. It was night and the picture was muddy. They saw the man walk out, carrying his bag, and get into a white compact car.

"Is that a Corolla?" Duncan asked.

"I think so," Eve said. "The design from four or five years ago."

"I was afraid of that. It's one of the most

common cars in Los Angeles and one of the most stolen cars in the country."

"You'd think people would rather steal Ferraris," Bert said.

"There's more demand for Toyota parts," Duncan said. "Please tell me you have a shot of the car's license plate."

Bert paused on the image of the Corolla leaving the frame. It was a bird's-eye view of the top of the car. "That's all we have."

"Damn," Duncan said. "We're going to need you to knock off a copy of that video. Can you print out a screen grab of your best shot of that guy's face?"

"Sure," Bert said. "Give me a couple of minutes."

Eve and Duncan walked out of the room and out onto the sales floor to wait. She hated the lighting in Walmarts. It made everything and everyone look like they'd walked through a downpour of urine.

"You came up with a great lead, Eve, and I'm sure that's our guy, but we're screwed."

"Why do you say that?"

"If we ask the DMV to spit out a list of every Corolla registered within, say, a five-mile radius of the crime scene, and if we check on every Corolla that's been stolen or recovered in LA in the last week, we'll still have to go through a thousand-plus hits," Duncan said. "Even if we draft everyone in the station and bring in reserve deputies to help us, it could take us weeks to find this guy. And what if the car is registered elsewhere in California or in another state? That's tens of thousands of white Toyota Corollas. We might never find him."

"We could release his picture to the media."

"That would be an absolute last resort. It would tell the guy that we are onto him and send him into hiding. It could also put the people around him in immediate danger. He might kill more people to cover his tracks. Right now, he probably thinks he's safe in plain sight, going about his business."

"He's not wearing gloves in those surveillance videos," Eve said. "Maybe we can pull his prints off the items in the shopping bag or from the basket of DVDs he sorted through."

"Don't get your hopes up. This isn't a TV cop show, where forensics solves everything in ten seconds using technology out of *Star Trek* and instant access to databases that don't actually exist. Lots of people have touched the products he bought along the supply chain, including whoever stocks the shelves here and the cashiers. We might get prints and we might not. This guy proved at the crime scene that he's forensically aware, thanks to those same fucking TV shows, by the way, so he probably wiped the stuff that he bought before he brought it in the house. As far as the DVDs go, hundreds of people have gone through that bargain bin. Even in the best of circumstances, we get usable prints maybe thirty percent of the time and only five percent of those end up identifying someone. The odds of us getting usable prints from this are about the same as aliens coming to Earth and making first contact with me."

The scab on Eve's head itched and she resisted the urge to scratch it. The last thing she needed was to break the scab and have to hide the blood in her hair again. But thinking about that gave her an idea. "I might have an easier way to find out who he is."

"Like what?"

"I'm not telling you yet because you're so negative," Eve said. "Have some faith."

"That's the first thing you lose doing this job," he said. "If you want to be any good at it."

# CHAPTER SIXTEEN

When they returned to the station shortly after 3:00 p.m., Eve went straight to her cubicle and searched through the stacks of papers on her desk. Duncan joined her a moment later, smelling like the McDonald's meals they'd eaten in the car on the way back and slurping on what was left of his large Coke. Biddle and Garvey were out in the field.

"What are you looking for?" he asked.

"I had some deputies log the make, model, and license plate numbers of all the cars parked at the Topanga Park trailheads." She found the reports and began sorting through them.

"That's a long shot."

"Not if I'm right about who attacked me on the hill." She yanked a paper from the pile and held it up to Duncan. "One of the cars at the trailhead was a white Toyota Corolla."

"Did the deputy interview the owner?"

"No, but he got the license plate." She turned to her computer, logged in to the DMV database, and ran the plate number. The details came up almost immediately. "The Corolla is registered to Beatrice Coyle, 4201 Topanga Canyon Drive, #A171."

Duncan dropped his cup, still half filled with

ice, into her trash can and looked over her shoulder. "That's the mobile home park on the way up Topanga, the one tucked into that sharp curve."

She was familiar with the trailer park. A few years ago, an elderly woman suffering chest pains pulled a gun on paramedics, who fled and called for backup. The woman sat on the patio of her trailer and held off a sheriff's department SWAT team for twenty-two hours. A crisis negotiation robot was sent in to make contact with her and she shot it twice, whacked it with a broom, attacked it with a drill, and threw a tarp over it. Even flash grenades and tear gas failed to dislodge her. She didn't come out until she was good and ready.

Eve pulled up Beatrice Coyle's personal details and her DMV photo. When the picture was taken, Beatrice was a sixty-seven-year-old lady with a stern headmaster expression and a purple beehive hairdo. She wore glasses with lenses thick enough to see the surface of Mars and a set of fake pearl earrings that looked like they were made out of jawbreakers.

"Beatrice Coyle died two years ago, but let's see if there are any other licensed drivers living at that address." Eve typed some more and hit pay dirt. "Her son, Lionel Coyle, age twenty-four."

"Let's see his face," Duncan said.

Eve clicked some more keys and his picture came up. It was the same guy they saw on the Walmart video.

Duncan held the printout of the video screen grab next to Eve's monitor just to drive the point home. "Hot damn. He's even got his mother's facial hair. I'll bring Crockett and Tubbs back in to work the databases. We've got to find out everything there is to know about Coyle . . . starting with where the hell he is right now."

"We can cruise by his home and see if the car is out front."

"Problem is, that mobile home park is a tight-knit community. Two seconds after we roll through, the entire place will know we were there, including Coyle. And if he's not around, then a neighbor might call him and warn him off."

"How about sending the chopper over?"

"We can, but those mobile homes are packed tightly together and most of 'em have carports. If his car is under one, we won't see it. And if he is there, a chopper circling overhead might spook him."

"I have a solution," she said.

"A drone?" he said.

"More old school than that."

"I like it already," Duncan said.

At the top of Topanga Canyon Boulevard, where it crested the hill, was an overlook that offered a spectacular view north over the smog-choked San Fernando Valley and beyond. A huge cloud of smoke from the Stevenson Ranch fire that Eve had passed that morning hung over the Santa Susana Mountains. A digital sign on a trailer, set up at the overlook by the forestry service, warned drivers on Topanga of the red flag warning in effect and the extreme fire danger. The Santa Anas were blowing hot and hard through the dry Santa Monica Mountains and one tossed cigarette could spark an inferno.

Duncan parked the plain-wrap SUV beside the digital sign and Eve pulled her bike out of the back. They'd swung by her condo earlier and she'd changed into a blue short-sleeve biking jersey, black cycling shorts, and wraparound racing sunglasses.

She placed her phone into a carrier on her handlebars, checked to make sure her Bluetooth earpiece was synced, and put on her helmet.

Duncan spoke into his phone. "Can you hear me?"

"Loud and clear."

"Are you sure he won't recognize you if he steps out to water his roses?"

"I'm wearing a helmet and sunglasses, which pretty much hides my face, and I won't be stopping to give him a good look at me anyway."

"Stay in touch," Duncan said.

She nodded, got on her bike, and headed down

the hill, something she'd done many times before. Biking in the Santa Monica Mountains was what she did whenever she had free time. In fact, it was how she'd ended up in Robbery-Homicide.

Eve had been riding downhill on a remote, winding two-lane stretch of Mulholland Highway when a Lamborghini Aventador roared around a curve and nearly ran her off the cliff. She spotted the car later in the parking lot of the Rock Store, a popular hangout with bikers.

Blake Largo was out of the car and wearing a ridiculous Bengal tiger polo shirt and velvet shorts and was berating a woman in a tight mini bandage dress who was teetering shakily on high stiletto heels. Eve later learned her name was Shirlee.

"You puked all over my Lambo!" Largo yelled.

"I'm sorry," Shirlee said. "All those curves made me carsick."

Eve got off her bike and approached the guy. She didn't know that Blake Largo was a celebrity and was unaware that a bunch of customers at the Rock Store were already capturing the scene on their cell phones.

"It'll cost me what you earn in a year to clean this up."

"I told you to slow down," Shirlee said.

Largo backhanded her across the face, nearly knocking her off her feet. "Nobody tells me anything."

Eve stepped between him and Shirlee. There

was no way she was letting this asshole hit the woman again.

"Back off," she said and looked over her shoulder at Shirlee. "Are you okay?"

The woman nodded, but her nose was bleeding. That was not okay as far as Eve was concerned.

"Who gives a shit about her?" Largo said. "Look at my Lambo. There's bitch puke all over the suede dash."

Eve turned back to Largo. "Shut up."

Largo took a swing at her. She dodged the blow, grabbed his arm, wrenched it behind his back, and forced him face-first to the ground, pinning him down.

"Apologize," Eve said.

"Fuck you," he said. Eve twisted his arm up until he winced. "I'm sorry! I'm sorry!"

"Not to me," Eve said. "To her. Say it like you mean it."

He looked up at Shirlee, who appeared stunned by the unexpected turn of events. His eyes became moist, his expression pleading.

"I'm sorry. There's no excuse for what I did. I hope you can find it in your heart to forgive me."

"Wow," Eve said. "You're good. I almost believe it."

"You should." Shirlee wiped her nose and sniffled. "He's got an Oscar. He keeps it by his bed and stares at it while he's fucking."

That was more than Eve wanted to know.

"Let me up," Largo said.

"Nope," Eve said. "I smell alcohol on your breath."

"So what? You gonna write me a ticket?"

"I would but I'm off duty." She turned to see the crowd of customers behind her, filming it all, and said to nobody in particular: "Someone please call the sheriff's station. Let them know that Detective Eve Ronin is holding a man in custody for assault and possible DUI."

And that was how she ended up where she was now.

The mobile home park where Coyle lived was tucked into a sharp curve of the two-lane road and was surrounded by trees and thick brush. She rode into the complex. There was a fountain at the entrance and, beyond that, a central clubhouse and pool.

"I'm inside," Eve said.

"Ten-four," Duncan responded.

Several narrow roads branched off from the entrance, each lined with well-tended mobile homes packed tightly together. She went down the road that Coyle lived on. She coasted past Coyle's place, a nicely tended mobile home with fake wooden siding and flower boxes filled with plastic flowers. He wouldn't be coming out to water those. The carport was empty.

"Nobody's home," Eve said and wondered if he'd fled for good.

"Is there anywhere we can sit and keep our eyes on the place without attracting attention from the neighbors?"

Eve rode to the end of the street, made a U-turn, and made another pass by the house. On her way down, she noticed a mobile home at the corner with a FOR SALE sign out front. One of the windows looked out at Coyle's place.

"Maybe," Eve said and continued out of the mobile home park and on down Topanga Canyon. "I'll meet you at Bristol Farms."

She turned left where Topanga hit Mulholland Drive, rode past the intersection with Mulholland Highway where the LAPD tried to scam them, and then past the Motion Picture and Television Country House and Hospital, where her father, Vince, lived in one of the bungalows on the forty-eight-acre property. Eve wasn't the least bit tempted to ride in for a reunion.

Instead, she entered the shopping center strip across the street and rode to Bristol Farms, a high-end grocery store, just as Duncan parked out front in the Explorer. She got off her bike and removed her helmet. He got out and opened the tailgate.

"There's a mobile home for sale on the corner of Coyle's street," Eve said. "If the Realtor will play along, maybe we can go in as a cleaning or painting crew and nobody will know we're cops."

He helped her lift her bike into the SUV. "That'll work."

"There's only one way in and out of the mobile home park and it's off Topanga Canyon, which is good. The bad news is we can't stake out the entrance without being seen."

"No problem. We'll plant unmarked units down at Mulholland Drive and more up on the overlook, so we'll have both ends of Topanga Canyon covered. We'll see him coming or going."

"If he's not already gone for good," Eve said.

"You'll feel more optimistic after you've had a couple apple fritters." Duncan gestured to the grocery store, which sold gourmet donuts in their bakery. "I always do."

# CHAPTER SEVENTEEN

She opted for Red Bull instead of an apple fritter and it definitely improved her mood and her alertness. It was a good thing, too, because Biddle and Garvey were in the squad room when Eve and Duncan came in at four thirty and she needed to be sharp and ready to respond quickly to whatever they had for her. They'd pounce on any sluggishness in her thinking as a sign she wasn't fit for the job.

"Isn't that your crime-fighting costume?" Biddle said, giving her tight-fitting Lycra biking outfit a once-over. "It would look better with a cape and a logo on your chest."

"And maybe a mask to hide your real identity," Garvey said.

Biddle gave him a chiding look. "Deathfist doesn't want to hide her real identity. She wants to be a YouTube star again."

Eve ignored the digs. "What have you two come up with so far on Lionel Coyle?"

Biddle answered. "He's never served any time, but he was arrested once during his fifth year in high school for jerking off in the stands while watching cheerleader practice. It happened again during his one and only semester at Pierce College. Both times no charges were filed and he was sent into counseling."

"Did you say fifth year of high school?" Duncan said.

"I did," Biddle said.

Garvey spoke up. "I checked with the credit reporting agencies and Social Security to find his current employer. He's a plumber with Mr. Plunger in Canoga Park."

That struck a chord with Eve, who started swiping through the kitchen crime scene photos on her phone.

"We had a patrol car roll past their office," Garvey continued. "His Toyota Corolla is parked in the lot. But he's probably out in the field in one of their vans. You know, the ones with the huge plunger mounted on the top."

"The 'I'll Never Get Laid' mobile," Biddle said.

"Their bread and butter is handling residential service calls for warranty companies," Garvey said. "He's probably out on calls until the end of his shift."

Eve found what she was looking for. There was a Mr. Plunger magnet on Tanya's refrigerator.

"Okay," Duncan said. "So we know where to find him and we can keep him under surveillance. That's nice. But we don't have anything on him. All we know is that he bought the same trash bags and cleansers at Walmart on Wednesday that we found in a Walmart bag in Tanya's house . . . and that he drives a white

Toyota Corolla just like one that was parked at the Topanga State Park trailhead on Thursday. Lots of people buy those same things at Walmart and drive Corollas. It's all circumstantial and it doesn't put him in the house. I'm not sure we have enough probable cause for a judge to grant us a search warrant."

"I am," Eve said. She held up her phone to show them the picture of the plunger-shaped refrigerator magnet with a local phone number on it.

"I got one of those on my fridge, too," Duncan said. "It doesn't mean Coyle has been in my house."

She lowered her phone and started dialing a number. "We can clear that up right now."

"Who are you calling?" Duncan asked.

She held up her hand in a "hold on" gesture and put the call on speaker.

"Hello, you've reached Mr. Plunger, what can I do for you?" a cheerful woman said.

"I'm hoping you can help me out," Eve said. "My neighbor is looking for a plumber and I wanted to recommend the nice young man you sent us a while back . . . but I've lost the invoice with his name on it."

"Sure, I can help you," Cheerful said. "What's your name and address?"

"Tanya Kenworth, 728 Saddleback Trail Court. It's down in Topanga."

"I love that area," Cheerful said. "Here it is. The plumber was Lionel Coyle."

The jolt of adrenaline that hit Eve's system was better than a six-pack of Red Bull. Eve shared looks with the three detectives, who were all smiling.

"Thank you," Eve said. "I'll make sure my neighbor asks for him when she calls."

She hung up. Everybody high-fived each other. For a moment, whatever resentment Biddle and Garvey had toward her disappeared and they all enjoyed the satisfaction of making a connection between their suspect and the victims. It was an inevitable discovery. Biddle and Garvey would certainly have contacted Mr. Plumber in the course of their own investigation to see if Coyle had serviced Tanya's home. But Eve jumped on it first and did so in a way that wouldn't tip off the suspect that the detectives were onto him.

"Let's get a warrant," she said.

"Yeah," Duncan said. "Can I have a word with you?"

"Sure," Eve said, wondering why he wanted to talk away from Biddle and Garvey.

He led her back to his cubicle and spoke to her in a hushed tone. "You're in charge, so I don't want to say something that might further undermine your tenuous authority over Crockett and Tubbs."

"I appreciate that," she said, wary now.

"I should be the one to walk the warrant through," Duncan said, meaning that he wanted to prepare the paperwork, present the case to the assistant district attorney, and then go with the prosecutor to see the judge.

"I'm the lead detective on this and I'm capable of writing a warrant."

"I'm sure you are and can do a passable job."

"Passable?"

"The fact is what we have on Coyle is bullshit."

"You just heard the call. Coyle was in her house."

"It feels great to establish *a* connection, but it doesn't feel nearly as good as *the* connection," Duncan said. "It's like the difference between masturbation and sex."

"I'm not following," Eve said.

"Just because Coyle fixed a leaky faucet in Tanya's house weeks ago doesn't mean he went back Wednesday and butchered her."

"I don't see how that applies to your masturbation and sex metaphor, but I get your point anyway. What does that have to do with you writing the warrant instead of me?"

"There are ways of writing it so it sounds like what we have constitutes strong probable cause."

"Then why are you complaining about the evidence?" she said. "Tell me what to say and I'll write it up."

"The problem is the ADA and the judge aren't

stupid and they won't really be fooled by great writing. But I have proven credibility that'll ease any doubts that they have. I'll sell it just by having this wrinkled bulldog face," Duncan said. "But if it's you who walks it through, they will see all the holes and question every conclusion."

"So you're saying we'll get the warrant because of your skill at smoke and mirrors and your established relationships with the ADA and the judge," she said. "It's not about my age, sex, inexperience, or notoriety."

"It's totally about your age, sex, inexperience, and notoriety."

"They can go fuck themselves," she said.

"Yes, they can and so can you. What's more important to you right now? Getting the search warrant or taking a stand on sexism, ageism, cronyism, and all the nasty isms in this big, cruel world?"

The answer was obvious.

"Get the warrant," Eve said. "I'll start the surveillance on Coyle."

"Good call," Duncan said.

# CHAPTER EIGHTEEN

It was five forty-five and dark out, so it felt a lot later than it actually was. It didn't help that Eve had only taken a short nap over the past two days.

She was parked in the Explorer on Deering Avenue in Canoga Park, facing the Mr. Plunger offices, a low-lying cinderblock box in the center of a cracked asphalt parking lot. The narrow street was in the center of an industrial neighborhood in the northwestern edge of the San Fernando Valley that had blossomed around a railroad line that was now long gone, replaced by a dedicated high-speed bus lane. The businesses on Deering included an electrical supply store, several collision repair shops, a roofing company, and a hardwood floor showroom.

A few Mr. Plunger trucks, impossible to miss with their giant plungers on top, had come and gone during her watch but Coyle's Corolla was still parked in the lot, so if he'd come back, he was still in the building.

Biddle was parked farther south, at the intersection of Deering and Saticoy, ready to trade off with Eve in tailing Coyle.

Garvey was already staked out in the empty for-sale mobile home across from Coyle's place.

Eve had gotten the lockbox code for it from the Realtor before she left the station.

Now all that was left for Eve to do was wait for Coyle and drink more Red Bull to fight the creeping fatigue that was threatening to knock her out. She was wearing her cycling gear and her bike was loaded in the back, all of which helped her look like a civilian if anyone happened to notice her sitting there.

Eve used the time to ponder the case. The evidence suggested that Coyle was already in the house on Wednesday morning when Tanya arrived. How did he get in? Perhaps with a stolen key. Or he'd unlocked or disabled a door or window when he was there doing a plumbing repair.

Why was he in the house? Perhaps it was a burglary and Tanya walked in on him. So he killed her . . . and while he was cutting her up, the kids came home, and he was forced to kill them, too.

But that scenario didn't explain why he brought a knife with him. Was it simply for protection in case someone was inside? Or perhaps it wasn't a burglary at all. Maybe he was waiting in the house for Tanya to come home so he could rape her. But if that was his intention, why did he stab her in the kitchen? Was it to guarantee that she wouldn't be physically able to fight him off when he dragged her to the bedroom? Did she put up a fight anyway? Was that why he was so furious when he stabbed her to death?

Maybe Tanya wasn't his target. Maybe it was Caitlin. But Eve thought there had to be easier ways to rape Caitlin than by murdering and dismembering her mother and killing her brother first. And if raping Caitlin was his goal, why did he slit her throat in the bedroom as she tried to escape?

Or perhaps it wasn't about burglary or rape. Maybe it was always about murder. He came to kill Tanya and then it all went to hell when the kids came back. Or maybe he'd always intended to kill them all, one by one, when they came home.

Or did Jared hire Coyle to get rid of the family that wouldn't leave his house?

There were too many possible scenarios, too many maybes.

What they were missing was a key piece of the puzzle, something that would make the picture start to emerge. If they already had that key piece, Eve was too tired to see it or reason it out now.

At the same moment Eve came to that conclusion, Lionel Coyle emerged from the building and got into his Corolla. She got on the radio and alerted Biddle that Coyle was on the move.

Coyle pulled out, turned right leaving the

parking lot, and headed south on Deering. Eve pulled out behind him. There was no other traffic on the street, so she stayed two car lengths behind him.

As Coyle turned right onto Saticoy, Biddle pulled in behind him and the two cars moved into the left turn lane at the intersection with Canoga.

Coyle headed south on Canoga for four blocks and then turned right on Sherman Way. At that point, Eve got behind him and Biddle lagged a few cars behind her. Coyle turned left into a parking lot beside a Kentucky Fried Chicken on the southeastern corner of Sherman Way and Topanga.

Eve continued on, turned left at Topanga, and pulled over into a Bank of America parking lot half a block down. Biddle parked on Sherman Way across the street from KFC.

She assumed Coyle was getting dinner and that he'd be heading south on Topanga afterward to go home. If she was wrong, Biddle would pick up the tail again and she'd catch up with them.

Coyle went into the KFC, came out a few minutes later carrying a takeout bag, and got back into his car. He drove out of the parking lot, turned left going westbound on Sherman Way, and then, on the yellow light, turned left onto southbound Topanga. Eve exited the Bank of America parking lot and slipped into traffic two cars behind him.

She alerted Garvey that they were on their way. Coyle headed down Topanga into the hills. Eve turned off at Mulholland Drive and Biddle followed Coyle until he went into the mobile home park. Biddle kept on going, pulling into the overlook farther up Topanga.

Garvey called in moments later to report that Coyle was in his house. Eve passed an unmarked LASD Crown Vic at the corner of Mulholland and Mulholland, manned by Deputy Ross in plain clothes.

She instructed the three men to keep an eye on Coyle and told them that she was headed back to the station to start slogging through the paperwork that needed to be done while they waited on the warrant. On the way to the station, Duncan called her.

"How's it going with Coyle?" he asked.

"He's at home and under surveillance. How's the warrant going?"

"ADA Burnside is doing a rewrite," Duncan said. "Then we have to find a judge. It will probably be another few hours until we get the warrant."

"I'll be at the station, writing up reports."

"I have a better idea. Go home, get some sleep. I'll call you if anything happens or the moment the warrant comes through."

"I need to be here," she said. "I have work to do."

"You haven't slept in two days," Duncan said. "You're setting yourself up for disaster. When you're that tired, you make bad decisions and your reaction time is shit. You could hurt the case or, worse, get me killed when I'm only weeks away from retirement. You know what a tragic cliché that would be?"

She knew he was right. "Okay. But call me the instant anything breaks."

Eve drove back to the station, unloaded her bike, and was riding out to Agoura Road just as Cleve Kenworth pulled into the parking lot in his Chevy Malibu. He was going too fast and his tires squealed as he came to a hard stop in the parking space. She pulled up beside his car as he kicked open his door and got out, his face as red as his bloodshot eyes.

"I heard on the radio coming down here that there's blood all over Tanya's house, and you're out searching the woods with dogs for my kids," he said in a loud voice. "Is that true?"

"Calm down, Mr. Kenworth. Let's talk inside."

"Fuck that," he said, stabbing a finger at her. "It's my kids who are missing and a Goddamn reporter and everybody in LA knows more about what's going on than I do. It isn't right."

Eve knew she'd made a big mistake. She'd told the public more than she'd told him. But it was a lot easier to talk to a camera than to a man who'd lost his family. So to spare herself discomfort, she'd jacked up his torture instead. It was a selfish, cruel thing to do and she couldn't understand how she had done it so easily, without a second thought or regret. Sometimes it felt like she was a stranger to herself.

"No, it isn't, and I'm sorry." The apology wasn't enough and she knew it.

"So answer the question," Cleve said.

"There's a lot of blood at the house. But we don't know who it came from yet. Your family wasn't there."

"You mean there were no bodies. Is that what the dogs are looking for?"

"They're looking for a trail that will lead us to your children," Eve said, baffled that, even now, she couldn't bring herself to tell him the truth. What was wrong with her? There was no hope and she wasn't sparing him any pain by implying that there was. In the end, she would just be hurting him more. But she'd done it again anyway.

"Did you know all that this morning when we talked?"

She nodded. "There are still a lot of unanswered questions right now and I'm—"

"Going on a fucking bike ride," he interrupted, his voice tinged with disgust. "Have fun."

"It's not what it looks like," she said, feeling as if she were standing in front of him naked instead of in her cycling wear. She had this ridiculous urge to cover her chest and crotch. "I was on surveillance. But that's not important. Here's what I know. There was some horrible violence in that house and your children are missing. It's unlikely that we are going to find them unharmed . . . but I'm trying to keep an open mind."

"You believe my children are dead but you won't know until you find their bodies," he said. "That's what you're telling me."

There it was. She'd made him say it because she couldn't. He had more guts than she did and she was ashamed, but still not enough to do the right thing when it counted.

"I'm very sorry, Mr. Kenworth."

He looked as disgusted with her as she was with herself.

"I'll be at the Good Nite Inn down the street until this is over." He turned his back on her, got into his car, and drove off.

She watched him go, then got on her bike and started riding home. It wasn't until she got to her door that she realized she'd been crying the whole way.

# CHAPTER NINETEEN

Eve was awakened the next morning by insistent knocking at her front door, followed by the distinctive ringtone of her iPhone. She reached out to her nightstand, picked up her phone, and looked at the screen. It said MOM.

She answered the call as she got out of bed in her T-shirt and panties. "I can't talk right now. There's someone at the door."

"It's me. You didn't hear my knocking so I called," her mom said. "Do you have a man over?"

"No," Eve said, reaching for her bathrobe.

"That's a shame." Her mom disconnected.

Eve checked the time on her phone as she went downstairs. It was 7:00 a.m. She'd been asleep for twelve hours and probably would have slept for a few more if not for the wake-up call. She quickly checked her recent calls to see if she'd slept through Duncan trying to reach her and was relieved to see that she hadn't. On the other hand, it meant the warrant still hadn't come through.

She opened the door and Jen Ronin bounded in, clutching a brown paper bag. Her mom was dressed in a vibrantly colorful, busy blouse from Chico's that looked like a Jackson Pollock painting and purple capri pants that could have been stolen from Mary Tyler Moore's dressing room on the original *Dick Van Dyke Show*. Jen was beautiful once, but too much bad plastic surgery gave her face the sculpted edges of a mannequin and a pair of hard, upright boobs to match.

"This place is like visiting the IKEA store only with less warmth and personality." Jen kissed her daughter on the cheek. "Would it kill you to put a picture on the wall?"

"I don't spend that much time here."

"I don't blame you. Prison cells are better decorated. I know. I was in one."

Eve closed the door. "Being an extra in a women-in-prison movie is nothing like a real prison."

"What do you know?" Her mom dismissed the criticism with a wave of her hand.

"I spent a year as a deputy at the county jail."

"Not in the Deep South, honey. It's a different world there. I was in a chain gang in a swamp. They don't have swamps in LA."

"You shot the movie in Burbank."

"Do you always have to argue with me about everything?"

Eve's shoulders were tensing up already. She didn't like the terse, uptight person she became when her mother was around but she couldn't help it. "What are you doing here, Mom? It's seven a.m. on a Saturday."

"I know you get up early on Saturdays to ride your bike and I was in the neighborhood."

"You live in Ventura." It was a beach community thirty miles northwest of Calabasas. Her mother rented a tiny apartment close enough to the ocean to smell it but not see it.

"I'm visiting your brother today and taking my granddaughter out for a manicure."

"She's four," Eve said.

"It's never too early to discover the secrets of beauty and marshal your feminine power." Jen took Eve's hand and regarded her short, unpolished nails. "She could teach you some things."

"Cops don't polish their nails."

"It would be a nicer world if they did. I brought you bagels and lox spread." Jen set her paper bag on the kitchen table and went into the kitchen. "Do they sell plates and knives at IKEA?"

"Sit down, Mom. I'll get it," Eve said and started gathering the plates and silverware. "But I have to get going soon. I'm in the middle of a case."

"I know all about it. I saw you again on TV. You were on every local channel." Jen opened the refrigerator and took out a carton of milk, checked the date, and brought it over to the table. "You're becoming a celebrity again."

"It's not intentional," Eve said and put a glass, a plate, and a knife in front of her mother.

"It's so easy for you." Jen reached into the bag and took out the plastic container of lox spread. "No effort required."

"I didn't mean it like that." Eve poured milk into their glasses.

"You don't appreciate the exposure you're getting," Jen said. "You never had to work for it."

"Because I don't want it, Mom. I'm not an actress or a model." Eve pulled an onion bagel out of the bag, set it on her plate, and sat down across from her mother. "I don't need the exposure."

"Not now, but you certainly used it to your benefit before," Jen said. She took an onion bagel for herself and began slicing it in half. "You can do it again."

"I got what I wanted and I'm where I want to be," Eve said, cutting her bagel, too. "It's not going to get me any further."

"Maybe not in the sheriff's department."

Eve put some lox spread on her bagel while she eyed her mother. "What are you getting at?"

"The studios and networks watch the news, you know. So do writers and producers." Jen picked up Eve's knife and used it to put lox spread on her own bagel. "What happened to you before, that was a moment, but what you're doing now, with this triple murder case, that's a story. They are going to see that. You could be in a series or a movie."

"I don't think so, but even if you're right, I'm not interested. I'm not going to cash in on this tragedy. That's not why I'm doing this job."

"You should talk to your father," Jen said.

Eve dropped her bagel and stared at her mother, who'd made that outrageous statement as casually as if they were discussing the weather. "You want me to talk to Vince, a man I haven't seen in ten years. Why would I do that?"

"He owes you years of unpaid child support," Jen said.

"I'm an adult now. It's not an issue anymore. What do you want me to do, arrest him?"

"I hadn't thought of that," Jen said. "That can be our fallback."

"Fallback?"

"He directed hundreds of TV shows before he retired and some of the baby writers he worked with then are big-time showrunners now. He could start paying back the child support by introducing you to some of them. If he doesn't, you'll put him in San Quentin, though it probably isn't much worse than where he is living now. Have you ever been there? The whole place reeks of adult diapers and breath mints."

Eve's shoulders were so tight that the rigidity was spreading up her neck, too. She'd have a bad headache soon if she didn't release some of the tension. She rolled her head and her shoulders but it didn't help.

"I know what you really want and you can forget it," Eve said. "You're too old to play me anyway."

"I know that. I'd be your captain," Jen said. "Tough, but sexy."

"I'm not going to sell myself as a movie or TV show and I sure as hell am not talking to Vince."

"Hollywood will be calling, and when they do, you can be ready with a writer, maybe even a script, and get this made on your terms," Jen said. "People wait a lifetime for an opportunity like this."

"You mean that *you* have," Eve said. "This is all about you trying to exploit me to make your own dreams come true."

"Why not?" Jen said. "If it wasn't for you kids, I could have become a star."

"What is that supposed to mean?"

"I couldn't have a career and be a single mother. So I chose motherhood over stardom."

"You're delusional," Eve said, her voice rising. "I raised Lisa and Kenny. I packed their lunches. I took them to school. I made their—"

"You love playing the martyr," her mother interrupted, dismissing her grievance with her signature wave, which only pissed off Eve more. "But I've seen this performance a thousand times and I know all of your lines."

Eve's phone rang in her bathrobe pocket. She took out her phone and answered it without looking at the caller ID. "Hello?"

"We just got the warrant," Duncan said. "We're staging in the Gelson's parking lot. I'll pick you up in five minutes."

*Thank God,* Eve thought, getting up from her seat.

"I'll meet you outside." Eve ended the call and faced her mom. "This has been a real treat but I have to go and search a man's home for pieces of the family that he butchered."

Jen smiled at her daughter. "Now *that's* a new line but it's still very much in character. You could play Joan of Arc."

Eve went upstairs to get dressed without saying goodbye to her mother.

# CHAPTER TWENTY

The Gelson's parking lot was only a few yards north of the **WELCOME TO CALABASAS** boulder on Mulholland Highway. On their way there, Eve strapped on her Kevlar vest and Duncan told her Coyle hadn't left the house.

"Why isn't the Special Enforcement Detail handling this?" Eve asked, referring to the LASD's SWAT unit, which was usually brought in on a warrant service when a suspect was likely to be armed and dangerous.

"They're tied up raiding a big meth lab in Palmdale."

Eve was glad they were busy. She wanted to be the first in the door on this one, not standing around outside waiting for SED to clear the place. But she frowned as if this development pissed her off, though she doubted that Duncan was fooled.

When they got to Gelson's, she could see a half dozen patrol cars were in the parking lot and a dozen deputies were standing outside, waiting for action. The CSU van was there, too, Nan and her team milling around it, sipping coffees from Starbucks.

Eve was out of the car before it came to a complete stop and approached the deputies, who gathered around her. A couple of them sniffled, fighting allergies exacerbated by the Santa Anas that were blowing through the mountains, spreading pollen everywhere.

"Here's the situation," she began. "We're serving a no-knock search warrant on Lionel Coyle. We believe he murdered and dismembered a woman, her two children, and their dog in a house up in Topanga but we haven't found the bodies."

"Jesus," one of the deputies said.

"A guy capable of that kind of brutality probably won't just smile and invite us in, especially if he has the bodies in his trailer," Eve said. "He could put up a fight, which is why we're authorized to do a dynamic entry."

That meant they would be breaking in the door instead of knocking on it.

Duncan spread a map of the mobile home park across the hood of a patrol car. "There's only one way in or out of the park, so sealing the place up tight won't be an issue. However, it's like a rat's nest inside. All the trailers and carports are packed real tight. The walls on these places are thin. Bullets start flying, or there are any fireworks, and there could be a lot of collateral damage."

"That's why we have to go in hard and fast," Eve said. "If we try to evacuate his neighbors first, even if we're on our tippy-toes, I believe he'll hear us coming and could hunker down for a long fight."

"A feeble old lady with a gun kept us up there for twenty-two hours," Deputy Clayton said. "I wonder whatever happened to that robot she shot."

"I heard it's an ATM in West Covina now," Deputy Ross said with a grin, "but it freaks out whenever somebody tries to deposit a Social Security check."

"PTSD is a bitch," Clayton said.

Eve didn't have the time or patience for banter. She tapped a spot on the map to focus their attention. "Coyle's place is right here."

The deputies gathered around to look. The trailer was on the northern edge of the complex, overlooking a steep slope of heavy brush below, and was sandwiched between trailers on either side.

"Four of us will take the door," Eve said. "Four others will surround the trailer in case he tries to make a break through a window or a trapdoor."

Eve spent the next few minutes going over the logistics and assigning deputies to keep people in their trailers and away from Coyle's place during the raid and for as long as it took to search his home and car afterward. Duncan volunteered to stay outside and handle crowd control during the breach.

Eve wasn't surprised but couldn't resist teasing

him. "Are you sure you don't want to go in with me?"

"Hell no. I'm retiring in a few weeks," Duncan said. "I'm not going to press my luck."

Eve shrugged and pointed to Ross. "Okay, you're with me. Let's do this."

The line of patrol cars surged into the mobile home park, splitting off and going up the various streets, while the last two vehicles blocked the opening to Topanga Canyon Boulevard.

Deputy Ross pulled in front of Coyle's carport, blocking the Corolla from leaving, and another patrol car rolled up from the other direction so they were nose-to-nose. Two more cars came up behind them. Eight officers emerged silently, guns drawn, Eve taking the lead.

Four deputies fanned out around the mobile home as Eve, Ross, and two others went up to the front door. One of the deputies came forward with a battering ram and, on Eve's signal, smashed open the door, which crumpled like it was a single sheet of aluminum foil.

Another deputy tossed a flash-bang grenade into the mobile home. They ducked back as the grenade exploded, throwing out blinding light and deafening sound but not shrapnel. The grenade was designed only to cause disorientation and not to create any damage.

The first two deputies spread right and left,

covering the two sides of the living room, while Eve and Ross went up the center toward the kitchen and the short hallway beyond.

Eve edged around the first door and spotted Coyle rising in bed, groggy and disoriented. She rushed up to his bed and whipped back the sheets with one hand to make sure he didn't have a weapon within reach. He was shirtless and wearing black boxers.

"Police. Show me your hands," Eve commanded. Ross was behind her, also targeting Coyle.

He raised his hands. Coyle was pale, with a few lonely hairs on his scrawny chest, his body dotted with several skin tags. She didn't see any cuts or bruises on his body that would indicate he'd been in a violent struggle. But nobody with a slashed throat, or multiple stab wounds in their torso, can put up much of a fight.

"Why are you here?" he asked, appearing dazed and confused. "What's going on?"

Eve said, "Stand up, face the wall, and put your hands over your head."

Coyle did as he was told, facing one of the *Planet of the Apes* movie posters and lobby cards that Eve now noticed were all over his walls.

Eve tossed his pillow aside, just to make sure there wasn't a gun underneath, then holstered her weapon. "Turn around slowly and keep your hands on your head."

Coyle did as he was told. Ross kept his gun trained on him. A different man faced them than the one who'd turned to the wall. In the intervening seconds, Coyle's grogginess had dissipated and he seemed unnaturally relaxed, even amused.

He smiled at Eve. "Good morning. It's always nice to wake up to a pretty face."

She wanted to punch his crooked teeth out. "I'm Detective Eve Ronin, Los Angeles County Sheriff's Department."

"I thought I recognized you. You're the Deathfist cop. I'm in my underwear and I've got a celebrity in my bedroom. It's a dream come true."

"We have a warrant to search your home and car."

"What are you looking for?"

"Evidence related to the assault and suspected murder of Tanya Kenworth and her two children, Caitlin and Troy."

"I don't know them and I've never hurt anyone in my life. I'm a lover, not a killer," Coyle said. "Can I get a selfie with you?"

There was a slimy, flirtatious tone to his remark, which she assumed was meant to sexualize and belittle her in some way. It wasn't working. All he'd managed to do was come across as creepy, which didn't help sell his innocence.

In the hallway, she heard a deputy report on his

radio. "We have secured the lone occupant and cleared the premises."

"Where were you on Wednesday and Thursday?" Eve asked.

Coyle made a show of thinking back, his hands still on his head. "I was home sick on Wednesday. Must have ate something on Tuesday that disagreed with me. Thursday was my day off. I felt better so I went hiking."

"Where?"

He looked her in the eye and his smile seemed to widen. "Topanga State Park."

It was clear that Coyle was well aware that Eve already knew that and it pleased him. She figured this was his way of gloating to her face about the beating he gave her on the hill.

"We're going outside," she said. "Keep your hands on your head until I tell you otherwise."

Coyle walked barefoot out of his room, his hands on his head. As they stepped out, Eve peeked into the other bedroom. It obviously belonged to his mother and seemed untouched since she'd died. It even smelled like perfume.

She followed Coyle and Ross down the hall, through the open kitchen and living room, and outside, where two more deputies were waiting.

"You can lower your hands," Eve said, confident that Coyle didn't present a danger to anyone right now. She saw the CSU van moving in. "Is there anything you want to tell us about before we start going through your house?"

"I didn't put the toilet seat down and I might not have flushed the last time I used it," Coyle said. "We're in a drought, you know, and I'm doing my part. I wasn't expecting guests. Sorry about that."

"Where are the keys to your car?"

"On the kitchen counter," Coyle said. "Oh, and if you're done admiring my physique, could you bring me some clothes?"

She liked that he wasn't comfortable being nearly naked in front of her and his second attempt to sexualize the situation didn't give her any incentive to make him feel any better. In fact, it encouraged her to prolong his discomfort.

Eve glanced at Ross. "Put Mr. Coyle in the back seat of a patrol car where he'll be warm and can protect his modesty."

# CHAPTER TWENTY-ONE

Eve went back into the house to start looking for evidence. The kitchen and living room were basically one space separated by a countertop. There was a pink easy chair, a bloated black vinyl recliner, a 1970s-era couch, an antique coffee table, and stacks of DVDs piled on the floor in front of a big-screen TV that was almost as wide as the trailer.

She went back to Coyle's bedroom and regarded his collection of *Planet of the Apes* posters and lobby cards as she put on her gloves. The artwork was all from the original movies from the late 1960s and early '70s, not the later remakes. It was still a kid's room and not a man's bedroom.

There was a T-shirt, jeans, and socks on the floor beside the bed and some loose change, half a roll of breath mints, and a wallet on the bureau. The mirrored sliding closet door was open a crack and Eve saw the toe of a hiking boot on the floor inside.

She slid open the door to get a better look at the boot but was distracted by what was hanging among the shirts and jackets inside: a big, furry ape suit, complete from head to toe. It didn't look like a real ape but rather one of the distinctive "ape men" from the original *Planet of the Apes* movie.

Now Eve knew that she actually saw a beast on the hill: it was Coyle in this costume. This proved it, but only to her, because she didn't tell anybody else what she saw up there. That was a mistake. Because she'd been afraid of being mocked, now the suit was simply a bizarre discovery rather than a key piece of evidence.

*Why did he come back for his sleeping bag in an ape suit? Was he wearing it when he was watching the house? Was he wearing it during the murders?*

"That's bizarre," Nan said.

Eve turned to see Nan standing behind her, all suited up in Tyvek and carrying a camera and an evidence collection case.

"Have you ever come across someone obsessed with apes before?" Eve asked, stepping aside to give Nan a better look at it.

"Nope, but I'm willing to bet my salary that there's traces of semen in that suit."

"Yuck," Eve said.

"But that's only hypothetical because I can't test it. An ape costume is not among the items listed in your warrant."

"Did you find any unidentified fibers at the crime scene that might have come from this costume?"

Although the ape suit wasn't explicitly covered in the warrant, the collection of fibers from the suspect's home that might match fibers collected at the crime scene was within the broad scope of the search.

"Not that I'm aware of," Nan said. "But we'll collect a fiber from it just in case."

Eve squatted beside the pair of hiking boots, picked up one of them, and showed Nan the tread. "Does this look familiar to you?"

"Yes, it does. These are definitely the same shoes the killer wore in Tanya's house, but that doesn't mean it's *the* shoes. We won't know until we examine them for any fluids or carpet fibers unique to the crime scene."

Eve set the shoe back down where she found it, stood up, and moved to the bureau, where she began opening drawers while Nan photographed the closet. The warrant gave them the authority to look for anything that might tie Coyle to the crime scene, from something as large and obvious as the murder weapon and bloody shoes to anything that might have belonged to the victims or come from the home, including blood, hair, fibers, and other material.

The top drawers were filled with underwear and socks. The bottom drawer was filled with small knickknacks and souvenirs of all kinds, including a Golden Gate Bridge key chain, a SpongeBob pencil eraser, a clamshell, a pearl earring, ceramic chopsticks, a pocket watch, a miniature Chinese teacup, a dream catcher earring, a Space Needle spoon, a gold tie clip, a hula girl shot glass, a mood ring, and a souvenir chip from the Berlin Wall.

"I've seen that earring before," Nan said, looking over Eve's shoulder.

"Which one?"

"The dream catcher," Nan said. "It's part of a set. There was one just like it in Tanya's bedroom."

"He kept it as a souvenir?"

"It's possible. If it's hers, we might be able to get her DNA from it."

Eve felt a flutter of excitement in her chest, not only because this could tie Coyle to the house, but it also cast everything in the drawer in a new light. Now she wondered where everything else in the drawer came from.

Nan read the expression on her face. "We'll take pictures of every item in the drawer and log it all."

"Thanks," Eve said.

"It's what we do," Nan said.

A thought occurred to Eve. She left the room, squeezed past another CSU tech in the hall, and went into the kitchen, where she started opening the cupboards and drawers. The pantry was full of canned foods, like chili and SpaghettiOs, boxes of sugary breakfast cereal, a canister of

Pringles, a box of Ritz crackers, and an opened box of Oreo cookies.

She opened the doors under the sink, took out the garbage can, and began carefully sorting through it. There were empty soft drink and beer cans, fast-food wrappers from Taco Bell, some fried chicken bones, and a greasy, torn box from KFC.

Duncan came up behind her. "Found anything?"

She put the garbage can back under the sink and stood up. "You need to go see Coyle's bedroom closet."

"What for?"

"I don't want to ruin the surprise."

He headed down the hall and she went into the living room, squatted down in front of the TV, and began examining his stacks of DVDs. His collection included a lot of porn, a lot of action movies, and every *Planet of the Apes* film, the *Planet of the Apes* TV series box set, and all the episodes of the *Return to the Planet of the Apes* Saturday morning cartoon.

She picked up his DVD of the first *Planet of the Apes* movie, the one starring Charlton Heston and Roddy McDowall. The box was worn and scratched. When she opened it up, the disc fell out, the clips that held it in place broken off long ago.

"Wow, an ape suit, that's a first," Duncan said, coming up beside her. "But being an ape freak isn't a crime. We need something that links him to the murders."

"The treads of his hiking boots match the prints CSU lifted from the scene and he has an earring that could be half of a matched set that belonged to Tanya."

"I was hoping for something more definitive like the knife, some bloody clothes, or a Hefty trash bag full of body parts." Duncan squatted beside her and picked up one of the DVDs off the floor. "I don't think *Gangbang on the Planet of the Apes* is part of the official canon, in case you were wondering."

"What I'm wondering is why I don't see the first *Planet of the Apes* DVD that he bought at Walmart. The only one here is this old one." Eve held up the box in her hand. "I also don't see the Doritos or the Ding Dongs. They aren't in the kitchen and the wrappers aren't in the trash."

"How about bananas? You'd think he'd have a bunch of those."

Eve ignored the remark. "You don't think it's odd that they aren't here?"

Duncan sighed and rose to his feet, one of his knees cracking. "He could have eaten the Doritos and Ding Dongs Wednesday night and tossed the wrappers with everything else he got rid of."

"What about the DVD?"

"He could have given it to somebody as a gift," Duncan said, rubbing his right knee. "Maybe there was a birthday at the office or something. You're focusing on niggly stuff that doesn't matter and you're missing the big picture."

"I've got a picture for you," Nan said. Eve and Duncan turned to see Nan carrying a tiny digital camera in her gloved hand. The camera was neon pink and made for a child, who'd decorated it with stickers of flowers and butterflies. "I found this under his bed."

Eve and Duncan went over to her.

"He's a little old for a toy like that," Duncan said.

"I don't think it's his." Nan turned the camera, showed the screen to Eve and Duncan, and pressed an arrow-shaped button that enabled her to scroll through the images.

There was Cleve in a bathing suit on a swim dock at a lake, throwing a jubilant Troy into the water . . . Troy licking a melting ice cream cone . . . Caitlin in a bathing suit, grimacing as a wet golden retriever shook itself off next to her . . . Cleve and Troy roasting marshmallows over a campfire.

Eve didn't need to see more. It was Caitlin's camera. It had to be.

She looked at Duncan. "Definitive enough for you?"

"It will do for now," he said.

She knew what he meant. The camera proved Coyle stole something from Tanya's house, but it didn't prove that he killed the family. But it was certainly enough to put him in a cell while they looked for more evidence.

"Can you hold up that camera for me?" Eve asked. Nan did as instructed and Eve took a picture of the camera with her phone. "Thanks. Please send me the photos from the memory card as soon as you can."

"I'll be glad to," Nan said.

Eve started to go and then had another thought. "I'd also appreciate a rush on the DNA test from that urine sample collected on the hill."

Duncan winced, and Eve knew immediately that she'd made some kind of mistake, but she didn't know what it was.

Nan lifted her chin and looked down her nose at Eve. "I got your message about the piss the first time you asked."

"I'm sorry—" Eve began, but Nan cut her off.

"My team is meticulous and thorough, Detective. That's why the evidence we collect is strong and holds up in court. We'll go as fast as we can, but when you rush, you make mistakes. I don't rush."

"Understood," Eve said, pocketing her phone.

"I'm aware of the urgency of every investigation and I'm capable of prioritizing the processing of the evidence that we collect accordingly."

"I didn't mean to suggest otherwise."

"Uh-huh," Nan said. "I'd appreciate it if you'd

hurry up and arrest the suspect. Oh, and when you do, be sure to read him his rights."

Eve held up her hands in surrender. "Point made."

Actually, the point had already been made three times before, but Eve feared Nan might go on to make it a fourth and fifth time if she didn't firmly declare defeat and display her submission.

Eve lowered her hands, walked outside, and went straight to the patrol car where Ross was standing guard over Coyle.

She opened the back door of the patrol car. "Get out."

Coyle got up and stood in front of the open door. "You didn't bring me something to wear. I feel naked out here like this."

"I'm sure you'd prefer your ape suit."

"That would be nice," Coyle said. "Be a good girl and go get it, then we can take a selfie."

"Should we use Caitlin's camera?" Eve asked. Coyle didn't have a comeback for that, though she waited one long second for one, looking him in the eye. "You're under arrest for the murders of Tanya Kenworth, Caitlin Kenworth, and Troy Kenworth. Turn around and place your hands behind your back."

Coyle did as he was told and Eve slapped on the cuffs.

# CHAPTER
# TWENTY-TWO

After Eve read him his rights, Coyle cheerily invoked his right to remain silent as if he were ordering a Happy Meal. She put him back in the patrol car but she didn't rush to have him taken to the station for booking. Duncan's comment about the evidence troubled her.

*It'll do for now.*

Eve went over to Duncan, who stood outside the door to the trailer. "Would you mind taking Coyle through booking and processing?"

"I'd be glad to," he said.

"But before you do, I'd like you to work your smoke and mirrors again on the ADA and a judge. Do you think, based on finding Tanya's earring and Caitlin's camera in his place, that you can get a warrant to swab Coyle's genitals for traces of DNA from his victims?"

"That won't be a problem. Are you thinking that Coyle raped Tanya and things got out of hand?"

She shrugged. "We don't have a motive yet for the break-in and murders. Rape could be it and her DNA could tie him physically to one of the victims if we don't find their bodies."

"At the very least, the swabbing process will

humiliate him, which might yield some benefits," he said. "You sure you don't want to be there for it?"

"I'm positive," she said. The swabbing procedure was performed by the jail nurse as part of typical rape kit protocol but the booking officer, meaning Eve or whoever she designated to take her place, would be present for the whole thing. Coyle would stand naked on a sheet of paper and be asked to brush and fluff his pubic hair. Anything that fell out would land on the sheet. If Coyle didn't brush vigorously enough to get some pubic hair to fall on the sheet, the nurse would have to do it. The sheet, with whatever was on it, would be folded up and put in a sealed evidence bag.

After that, the nurse would swab Coyle's penis, inner thighs, legs, arms, and torso with large Q-tips. The inside of his mouth would also be swabbed, primarily to obtain his DNA, but sometimes a victim's DNA could be picked up if he licked or bit the victim. Blood and hair follicles would also be taken from Coyle. All of that would go into evidence bags, too.

"While you're supervising the swabbing," Eve said, "I'm going to do some more investigating."

"Wise decision," Duncan said. "Without the bodies, we're going to need a lot more evidence to make those charges stick."

At least she had some time to work. Arresting

Coyle on a Saturday morning meant the judicial system would move a lot slower for him than it would if she'd arrested him on a weekday. The courts and other city, state, and county offices were either completely closed or barely staffed on the weekend. Coyle wouldn't be arraigned until Monday. And, if he chose a public defender, he wouldn't see a lawyer until then, either.

"Maybe the search parties in the park will find something," Eve said.

"I wouldn't count on it. Coyle could have dumped those body parts anywhere," Duncan said. "I'll go get started on the warrant."

Duncan walked to his car and she thought about what he'd said about the bodies. The kids were probably killed around 3:00 p.m. Wednesday and Coyle went to Walmart at 10:30 that night. In between, he dismembered the children, did some "cleaning" at the house, and realized he needed to go shopping for more supplies. He wasn't going to show up covered with blood. That meant he had to shower and change first, either in the bloody bathtub at Tanya's house, in his own home, or somewhere else. Whether he disposed of the bodies before or after the Walmart trip, and her money was on before, she didn't think he had time to go very far. The bodies were within their jurisdiction, she was certain of that.

They already had cadaver dogs searching the park, but there were other local places to check out. For starters, there was the Calabasas landfill on Lost Hills Road, in the graded hills directly across from the sheriff's station north of the Ventura Freeway. That's where the bags of body parts would be if he'd tossed them in any local trash can or dumpster. But he also could have gone to the dump himself.

Eve spotted Biddle and Garvey chatting with a couple of deputies, made eye contact with the two detectives, and motioned them aside. They joined her.

"We've got to find those body parts," Eve said. "I need you to arrange a search of the Lost Hills dump and get some divers to check out Malibu Lake."

"How about getting a search party into Malibu Canyon along Las Virgenes?" Biddle said, referring to the deep gorge that cleaved the Santa Monica Mountains between Calabasas and the sea. Las Virgenes Road was cut into a mountainside along the ravine and was a scary drive along the edge for anyone afraid of heights. "He could have tossed the bags there. Cars can go off the cliff and not be spotted for years."

"We worked a case like that," Garvey said. "A wrecked Benz with two skeletons was found by firefighters putting out a small brush fire.

The bodies belonged to an elderly couple that had been missing for five years. Turns out their kids drove by their corpses every day without even knowing it. That's some haunting shit. It'd make a great movie. I've been pitching it around."

There was also the scandalous case a few years back of a woman who was released from custody at Lost Hills station very late one night and then disappeared. Her bones were found in the canyon years later but the details of her fate were still a mystery, as well as a continuing source of bad publicity for the department, thanks to an ongoing lawsuit from her family. Eve doubted Garvey was pitching *that* story to Hollywood.

"Go ahead and get a search going there," she said. "Any place you can think of is worth checking out. Don't wait to run it past me."

"Don't worry," Garvey said. "That's the last thing we'd do."

She let that go. "Also do a deep dive into Coyle's background. There might be something there that will help us. We need as much evidence as we can get before he's arraigned on Monday."

"We'd like to get some sleep first, if you don't mind," Biddle said pointedly. "We've been up all night watching Coyle's place."

"Right, of course, sorry," Eve said, embarrassed that she hadn't thought of that. "Let me hitch a ride with you back to the station and then you can go get some rest."

When they got back to Lost Hills, Biddle and Garvey got out and told her they'd be back in a few hours. She took the keys to their Crown Vic and drove out to Mr. Plunger in Canoga Park.

Eve knew the woman behind the counter was the cheerful voice on the phone the instant she saw her. The woman had a wide-eyed, wide-faced, wide-smiled exuberance that made Eve glad there was a counter between them— it lessened the chance that she would get an unwanted hug. On the wall beside the woman was a big map of the western San Fernando Valley and the communities in and around the Santa Monica Mountains. The map drew Eve's immediate attention. There were big black-line boundaries drawn on it with a Magic Marker designating Mr. Plunger's service area: the 118 freeway to the north, Las Virgenes Road to the west, Winnetka Avenue to the east, and south all the way to the Pacific Coast Highway. As far as Eve was concerned, that was also the search parameters for the bodies.

"Hello, I'm Brandy," the woman said with a big smile that showed off her perfect teeth, giving Eve a painful flashback to her own teenage orthodontic hell of braces and rubber bands. "How can I help you?"

Eve flashed her badge. "I'm Detective Eve Ronin, Los Angeles County Sheriff's Department. One of your plumbers, Lionel Coyle, has become a person of interest in a missing person investigation. I need to get the names and addresses of all of his service calls for the last twelve months."

"Sure thing," Brandy said, turning to her computer terminal. "I'll print it right out for you or I can email it to you."

Eve was startled by the immediate positive response. She'd been expecting at least a little pushback on her request.

"How about both?" Eve set her card on the counter. "My email address is on the card."

"Will do." Brandy took the card and gestured with a nod to a corner of the room. "Help yourself to some popcorn while you wait."

There was a movie theater–style popcorn machine on wheels in the corner of the room. The popcorn looked like it had been there for weeks and the glass was smeared with oil.

"No thanks," Eve said. "Do your service vehicles have GPS that allows you to track where they are and where they've been?"

"We aren't real high-tech around here. Our drivers call in when they arrive at a job and again when they are leaving it. That's how we know when and where to send them out on their next call."

"Have you had any complaints about Lionel Coyle?"

"Nope," Brandy said, getting up and walking back to a printer, which was spitting out pages. "The opposite, actually. People seem to like that he's friendly, he smells good, speaks English, and you don't see his hairy butt crack when he squats down or bends over."

There was a local plumbing company that advertised incessantly on LA radio and TV as "the Smell Good plumber," so the qualities that mattered to Mr. Plunger's customers weren't entirely a surprise to Eve.

"We actually do a bend-over test before we hire anybody. We have a strict no-butt-crack policy."

"That should be your motto," Eve said.

"Mr. Plunger, the No-Butt-Crack Plumber," Brandy said with delight. "I like it."

She handed the printout to Eve. It was a spreadsheet with nearly a thousand names and addresses, arranged by date. The number of service calls made sense to Eve. If Coyle worked six days a week, and saw three people a day, and he got a week off each year, that would be around nine hundred calls. There were no service calls last Wednesday or Thursday.

"Thanks for your help." Eve headed for the door.

Brandy called out after her. "Will Lionel be coming in to work on Monday?"

"I doubt it," she said.

"How long will he be away?"

"I'm guessing twenty-five years to life," Eve said.

# CHAPTER
# TWENTY-THREE

Eve went back to the Lost Hills station, read the email from Brandy at Mr. Plunger, and opened up the attached spreadsheet of Coyle's service calls for the last twelve months.

The list was organized by date. She reorganized it by address and saw that Coyle had visited Tanya's house twice, both service calls booked through Jared's home warranty policy insurance carrier. The first call, six months ago, was to fix a leaking pipe under the kitchen sink. The most recent visit was only a week before the murders to fix a leaking toilet. That worried Eve. It meant if any of Coyle's DNA was found in the kitchen or bathroom, his defense attorney could say it was left during the service calls, not the murders.

She wanted to cross-reference all of the homes or businesses Coyle visited as a plumber, and the people who lived or worked in those places, to the sheriff's department database to see if there were any crimes, arrests, patrol calls, or miscellaneous field observations at those same addresses. Miscellaneous field observations were the notes deputies made, and later filed in the database, whenever they saw something suspicious or stopped a suspicious individual without taking any action.

Eve was especially interested in "dead on arrival" burglary reports. During her time in burglary, the bulk of her reports fit that category. They were the cases when a homeowner was certain somebody had stolen items from their home, but there were no signs of a break-in. On top of that, they couldn't say what day the item went missing, only the day they first noticed it was gone, and therefore couldn't point to a specific service worker, like a cleaning lady or electrician, as the culprit. More often than not, it was likely the homeowner simply misplaced the item that they were certain was stolen. But she had a feeling the seemingly worthless items in Coyle's bottom drawer could be souvenirs stolen from homes he visited.

It would be laborious and time consuming for Eve to cross-reference the list herself, inputting one address at a time into the search box in the database. But fortunately, she knew that the LASD's Crime Analysis Unit had different resources and could probably do it within a few hours. The CAU was made up of civilian techies who loved to prove how useful, thorough, and revealing the information in the database could be to law enforcement and how fast they could deliver it. They also saw delivering thorough, high-value responses in "granular" detail as an incentive to get detectives and deputies, who hated paperwork and loathed the boxes they had to fill in on the online forms, to put as many facts as possible into the data they inputted into the system.

She emailed the list to CAU and followed up by immediately calling one of the techies there, Sue Trowbridge. Eve told Sue that she was working a triple-murder case, had a suspect in custody, and needed the information as fast as possible to make sure he didn't get back on the street.

"I'm a big fan of the red velvet cake at Nothing Bundt," Sue said.

"Are you asking for a bribe?" Eve asked lightheartedly.

"I'm asking for a reward. There's a subtle difference."

"You got it," Eve said. "I'll throw in a Chocolate Turtle bundtlet if I get the info in two hours. It's the flavor of the month."

"Deal," Sue said. "And I'm not going to ask how you know what their flavor of the month is."

Eve hung up the phone and used the wait time to start filling out reports, doing her part to add to the database and performing the drudgery necessary to get the wheels of justice turning.

Forty-five minutes later, Duncan wandered over to her cubicle. "I'm going on a donut run. You want anything?"

"No thanks," she said. "How did it go with Coyle?"

"That's why I need to fortify myself with a glazed old-fashioned. We got the warrant for the swab and I had to witness it. Watching a poor nurse brush the stinking pubes around an ape-loving psychokiller's junk is not an experience I'm gonna miss in my retirement."

"Did Coyle say anything?"

"Not a word," Duncan said. "Are you thinking of having a go at him?"

"I want to be better armed when I do," Eve said.

"You onto something?"

"I might be," she said. "I'll let you know if it pans out."

"When I get back from my donut run, I'll check in with the search teams, see what ground they've covered and where they plan to go next," Duncan said. "But we would have heard something if they'd found anything."

She nodded and got back to work. Thirty minutes later she got a call from Trowbridge at CAU.

"I've emailed you the matches," Trowbridge said.

*There were matches.* Eve felt a chill go down her spine. "You're amazing. You've earned two bundtlets."

"Our pleasure, Detective. Go get the bastard."

Eve opened up her email from Trowbridge. Each match listed the address, the crime, the date of the crime, and a wealth of other information, including links to the reports filed by the investigating officers or detectives. There was almost too much information. She quickly dismissed crimes, both major and minor, committed by the people living in those homes or businesses, including disturbing the peace, domestic abuse, drug possession, traffic violations, and nonpayment of child support.

That left crimes against the homeowners. She set aside crimes that had been solved, including one arson and two burglaries. That left three unsolved burglaries and a rape. Two of the unsolved burglaries were break-ins that seemed to have been committed by more than one person at a time and large amounts of cash and jewelry were taken. In one case, the burglars were captured on security camera video. She dismissed those two cases as well.

All that remained were a burglary and a rape.

The burglary case was a DOA report out of Calabasas, an elderly woman who was convinced she was burglarized even though there were no signs of a break-in and nothing valuable was taken. That could either be forgetfulness, to put it kindly, or a promising lead. Eve would check that one out.

And, finally, there was the rape. A young

woman in West Hills walked in her door from work and was raped by a man who was waiting in her home. He was wearing a monster mask and held a knife to her throat. No arrest was made in the case and no DNA was collected. But Eve was still intrigued by the parallels between the unsolved rape and her case, especially with the tenuous Coyle connection. Rather than read the report, Eve decided to call the investigating detective, who worked out of the Sex Crimes Division downtown, to find out more.

The detective answered on the first ring. "Sex Crimes. Macahan."

"This is Detective Eve Ronin, RHD out of the Lost Hills station."

"The Deathfist," he said.

She kept talking as if she hadn't heard him say that. "I'm working a triple homicide and you investigated a rape case that might connect with mine."

"You're working a triple homicide," he said. "Let me ask you a question. Before this, what was the biggest case you investigated?"

"I'm not doing this dance, Detective. A woman and her two children were murdered and dismembered in her home. I think I've got the guy who did it sitting in a cell here. You can help me keep him there by talking to me about a case or you can help him walk by wasting my time with bullshit. What's it going to be?"

He sighed. "What's the case of mine?"

"It was a rape, eight months ago, in West Hills. The victim's name was Vickie Denhoff. What can you tell me about it?"

"It was a heartbreaker. Denhoff is in her early thirties, lives alone, and is an accountant for an insurance company in Warner Center. She wasn't feeling well so her boss let her go home early. She walked in her house, went to her bedroom, and some guy in a mask jumped her from behind, put a knife to her throat, and told her he'd cut her if she screamed or didn't do exactly what he told her. To prove he was serious, he sliced her just deep enough to draw blood. He forced her onto the bed and raped her."

"The man was already in the house when she came home?"

"That's right."

"Was there any sign of a break-in?"

"Nope."

"Did she describe the mask he was wearing?"

"Only that it was a monster mask that covered his head completely," he said. "She closed her eyes through most of it."

"Were you able to collect any DNA?" She knew from browsing the report that the answer was no, but she wanted to know why.

"Have you ever seen that TV show *Monk*, about that uptight detective who is a clean freak and wants everything to be even?"

"He had OCD." [P SEP]

"Yeah, well, she's like him. Can't stand dirt. So the moment he was gone she didn't just shower and douche, she did it five or six times, completely disinfected herself, washed her clothes and her sheets before throwing them out, cleaned her entire house, and then called the police. I understand why she did it, of course, but she went to such an extreme that she virtually guaranteed we'd never be able to convict anyone for the rape. Vickie was victimized twice—first by the rapist and then by her own phobias. I felt terrible for her."

"She still might be able to help put him away," Eve said.

"You think your guy is her rapist?"

"There's a connection. He was a plumber who did a service call in her house a few weeks prior to the rape."

"That could be a coincidence."

"There's also a lot about the two cases that's similar. In both cases, he was waiting in the house for the victims, he had a knife, and there were no signs of a break-in. We also found an ape suit in his closet."

"An ape suit," Macahan repeated.

"Full body. Have you ever come across that before?"

"Rapists who wear animal costumes? Yeah, I've seen that before. I arrested a guy who

184

dressed up like a bear and raped little boys. The rapist admitted to me, to prove that he was just a normal guy with normal urges, that he was part of a group of software designers that held furry parties."

"What are furry parties?"

"Gatherings where everybody dresses up as animals and jerk off. One of the other guys at this furry party dressed up like a dog and had three Labradors at home that he sexually abused. We arrested him for bestiality. Here's a fun fact: I read a study about furries—people who get off wearing animal costumes—and the researcher says that twenty-five percent of 'em believe they aren't entirely human and wish they could become completely inhuman."

She was glad she didn't have Macahan's job. "Sounds like the guy you caught, and the one I have in a cell, succeeded in that goal."

"If you clear the Denhoff case with yours," he said, "I'll owe you one, Deathfist."

"You can start by calling me Eve."

"Let's wait and see if you pull off the doubleheader."

# CHAPTER
# TWENTY-FOUR

Esther Sondel was a widow in her mideighties with some kind of bone disease that had nearly bent her in half. But she still spent two or three months a year traveling around the world.

"I may not have the body I once had," Esther had told the LASD detective who'd taken her initial burglary report, "but I still have my head."

The comment made such a strong impression on the detective, or amused him so much, that he'd put it in his report. It was Esther's way of saying she wasn't senile and the things that were missing from her house were stolen, not misplaced. They weren't particularly valuable things in terms of financial worth but were rich in memories. She'd returned from one of her trips, noticed some trinkets were gone, and called the sheriff's department.

That's what had brought a detective to her duplex on Park Sorrento in Calabasas eight months ago and why Eve was back today. Esther lived on Calabasas Lake, a private park that was home to ducks and notoriously aggressive geese that were so violent, deputies were often called by irate homeowners wanting the fowl shot. The Calabasas Park Homeowners Association, wary of lawsuits from their notoriously litigious residents, erected signs around the lake warning people not to piss off the birds.

"This is a surprise," Esther said, leaning on her gnarled carved-wood cane as she led Eve out onto her patio overlooking the lake. She was Gandalf without the beard. "I thought you'd written me off as a senile old bat."

"Not at all," Eve said. "There just weren't any leads for us to pursue."

They sat down at one of the tables. "So what has changed?"

"I'd like you to browse through these photos and tell me if you recognize any items," Eve said, passing her phone across to Esther. Nan had sent Eve all the pictures of everything in Coyle's bottom dresser drawer. "Do you know how to swipe?"

"Infants who can't even talk yet can use iPads and iPhones," Esther said. "What makes you think I can't?"

"Sorry," Eve said.

Esther swiped rapidly through the photos with a knobby arthritic finger for a minute or two, then froze.

"What is it?" Eve asked.

Esther's finger trembled over the screen.

"In the summer of 1975, my husband and I were driving through France in this horrible little Citroën. Our car broke down in some village in

187

the middle of nowhere. We had no money, so we stayed in a room above the mechanic's garage overnight while he fixed our car. My daughter was conceived that night." She turned the camera to show Eve the picture. It was a leather key chain with the Citroën logo, two chevrons, on a metal medallion. "We kept this as a memento."

Eve's suspicion was now confirmed. Coyle's bottom dresser drawer was full of objects that he stole from the homes that he'd visited on service calls. Most of the knickknacks weren't overtly valuable. They were personal trinkets that he could slip into his pocket and that could go missing, without being noticed by the owners, for days, months, or even years.

The items didn't prove he was anything more than a thief but they raised important questions. Did he steal the items on his service calls? Or did he come back later, when nobody was home, and keep the items as souvenirs of his secret intrusions? If so, did Tanya catch him in the act? Was that the reason for his homicidal fury?

Now Eve was even more interested in showing Coyle's collection of knickknacks to Vickie Denhoff, the rape victim, to confirm her suspicions about his activities.

"Will I get this back?" Esther asked.

Eve nodded. "But it might be a while."

"I can wait," Esther said. "I intend to take it with me when I go."

"Go where?"

"To the grave, dear," Esther said. "I'm taking my wedding ring, the key chain, the first love letter Ira wrote to me, and the mink he bought me that I can't wear in public anymore."

# CHAPTER
# TWENTY-FIVE

Vickie Denhoff lived in a decades-old one-story ranch-style home on Julie Lane in West Hills, which was once the western-most edge of Canoga Park until it split off into its own community in the late 1980s. The corner of West Hills that Denhoff lived in was under LASD jurisdiction, while the rest of the community fell under the LAPD's protection.

The exterior of the house was clean and meticulously maintained. The lawn was so perfectly manicured and green, and the bushes so symmetrically trimmed, that Eve had to touch grass and the leaves on her way to the front door to be sure the landscaping was real and not plastic.

Eve had called ahead to make sure Vickie was there and so she'd be emotionally prepared for the questions she might be asked. Vickie opened the door so quickly, Eve suspected she'd been standing at the peephole watching her approach.

"Detective Ronin?" Vickie asked. She wasn't the OCD cliché that Eve was expecting, which was a socially awkward, demure woman with a severe haircut and wearing bland but perfectly pressed clothes that were buttoned up to the neck and didn't show any skin. She wore a loose-fitting navy-and-white gingham sundress, scoop necked with thin shoulder straps that showed off her shoulders and cleavage. Her curly blonde hair was styled in a simple messy bob.

Eve flashed her badge. "Thank you for seeing me on such short notice, Ms. Denhoff. I'm sorry to intrude on your Saturday afternoon. This won't take long."

"Please call me Vickie." She stepped aside and let Eve in. The house, unlike Vickie, did fit the cliché. It was impeccably clean, not a speck of dust or anything out of place. The furniture and artwork were all centered in relation to the walls behind them and the pieces evenly spaced. It looked like a furniture store or a display of some kind rather than a place where a person lived and relaxed. "What can I do for you?"

There was a hesitancy in Vickie's voice that Eve could sympathize with. Vickie was wary of opening old wounds.

"As I said on the phone, I'm investigating a case that could be related to yours, but I'm not going to ask you to go back over everything again. I'd just like you to look at some pictures and tell me if you recognize any of the items." Eve took out her phone and held it out to her.

Vickie regarded the screen, which was smudged with greasy fingerprints, and frowned. "Let's sit down. You can scroll through the pictures and I'll stop you if I see something I recognize. Is that okay?"

"Of course," Eve said, feeling stupid for not cleaning her dirty phone before offering it to a germophobe. They sat down side by side on the couch and Eve slowly swiped through the photos of the things in Coyle's drawer. They went through about two dozen items before Vickie said something, her eyebrows arching with surprise.

"That's mine." She pointed to a picture of a miniature teacup.

"How do you know?"

"It was part of a four-piece tea set that was in a huge antique dollhouse that belonged to my mother. The dollhouse is long gone, but I kept the tea set on a bookshelf in the guest room where my mom stays when she visits. One day, I noticed a teacup was gone."

"Was this day before or after you were attacked?"

"After," she said, her voice a little shaky. "Two weeks after. My mom came to stay with me when I was recovering. When I was cleaning up the room prior to her arrival I saw that the cup was gone. It really threw me. I mean, what was I supposed to do? There was no way I could replace the cup before Mom got here and I couldn't leave it like that. I had no choice but to remove one of the cups and hope for the best."

"I don't understand," Eve said. "Why did you remove a cup?"

"So there would be two cups left instead of three," Vickie said. "What would Mom think if she saw the room in disarray? She'd be even more concerned about me than she already was. The two cups worked out fine while she was here. She was too busy fussing over me to care. But after she left, I couldn't live with it. Two cups would have been fine for anybody else who didn't know they were part of a set. But I knew. I couldn't fool myself and so I ended up throwing them all away."

Eve nodded, not because she thought what Vickie did was the common sense thing to do but to buy herself some time to decide whether to show her one more photo, one that could cause her some pain.

Vickie asked, "Where did you find my cup?"

"We found it in the home of a man we believe attacked another woman," Eve said and made her decision. "There's another picture I'd like to show you."

Eve went online and found a headshot of actor Roddy McDowall in his ape makeup from *Planet of the Apes*. "Is this the monster mask your attacker was wearing?"

She showed Vickie the photo. Vickie stared at it analytically, showing no emotional reaction.

"It could be but I can't be sure," she said,

unconsciously touching the spot on her throat that had been cut with the knife. There was no visible scar there but Eve was sure there was one that Vickie could feel. "My memory of it is blurred. All I know was that it wasn't a human face. I closed my eyes and didn't open them again until he was gone."

Eve certainly understood that and had no interest in bringing back more bad memories for her. She pocketed her phone and stood up. "Thank you, Vickie. You've been a big help."

Vickie rose to her feet and walked Eve to the door. "Do you think this is the same man who raped me?"

"I think it's very likely," Eve said.

"Do you have him in jail?"

"Yes, I do."

"Keep him there." Vickie opened the door. "I might be able to start sleeping at night with the lights off again."

# CHAPTER TWENTY-SIX

Eve stopped at the Commons, an outdoor shopping center in Calabasas that was meant to evoke a quaint French village, and got a sandwich and coffee at Le Pain Quotidien, which she ate at a table outside under the shadow of a clock tower that held the world's largest Rolex. She'd never been to France, but she doubted many villages had Rolex clock towers.

It was 5:00 p.m. and beginning to get dark. Her phone vibrated. Eve picked it up and saw that Nan had sent her the photos from Caitlin's camera. She downloaded them and texted Nan.

How much longer are you going to be at Coyle's place?

Nan texted back.

Another hour or so.

Eve replied that she was on her way over to get the rundown and asked if there was anything she could bring her.

Nan asked for a Caramel Coconut Iced Latte

from Coffee Bean, which was at the shopping center across the street from the Commons. Eve said that would be no problem.

She got a couple of the iced lattes and headed up to the mobile home park, where she saw that there was still a crowd of people, most of them tenants of the park, standing outside the yellow police tape watching the CSU team do their work at Coyle's place.

Eve parked her car, got out with the two lattes, and closed the door with her hip. She handed one of the drinks to Deputy Clayton, who lifted up the yellow tape for her.

"You just became my nominee for detective of the year," he said.

"Do you ever take your sunglasses off?" she asked.

"Did the Lone Ranger ever take off his mask?"

She smiled and continued on to Coyle's mobile home. Nan met her outside the carport. Another CSU tech was on his knees outside the open driver's side door of Coyle's Toyota, taking samples from the carpet. Eve handed Nan the latte and she took a big sip.

"Thanks, I've been craving this all day," Nan said. "What do I owe you?"

"I'll settle for a single piece of evidence linking Coyle to the murders of Tanya Kenworth and her kids," Eve said and got a frown from Nan, indicating they'd come up with nothing so far. "Don't tell me that. What about the work boots?"

"They are the same brand and style of work boot but not the actual ones that he wore at the scene. This pair is brand new and they've never been worn, at the crime scene or anywhere else. These were his spares."

"Spares?"

"He has three pairs of the same Nike running shoes, two that are still in boxes and one that he's wearing regularly. My guess is that he waits for sales and then he buys multiple pairs of the shoes he likes."

"What about the carpet and floors? Surely he tracked some blood, cleanser, and motor oil into his house."

"I won't be one hundred percent certain until we get the samples back to the lab, but there doesn't appear to be any trace evidence from the crime scene in his house. We've checked everything, including the drains in the shower and sinks. Speaking of which, we also checked the drains at Tanya's house and we didn't find any hairs that match his."

Eve motioned to the Toyota. "You must have found something in his car."

Nan shook her head again. "It's clean."

It was frustrating and infuriating. "So he thoroughly scrubbed his car down after the killings."

"Definitely not," Nan said. Eve was confused and Nan could see it on her face. "When I said it was clean, I meant we haven't found any blood, body fluids, bone fragments, or anything else connected to the crime scene. But outside of that, the car is filthy. See for yourself."

Eve turned and looked at the car. It was covered in dirt and there was bird crap on the trunk lid and back window. The car obviously hadn't been washed in weeks. It didn't make any sense to her. If the car was clean, how did he get the trash and body parts out of the house? If his mobile home was clean, then where did he go to change his clothes and wash the blood off himself before going shopping at Walmart?

Despite all the evidence pointing to Coyle, there was still a big hole in the narrative, something she hadn't found, or couldn't see in front of her, that would explain it all and prove him guilty. Unless she figured out fast what it was, Coyle could be bailed out on Monday and only face a burglary charge.

One thought occurred to her. She took out her phone and called Mr. Plunger. Brandy answered cheerfully, as usual. "This is Detective Ronin again. I have a quick question. Are your plumbers allowed to take the service vehicles home with them?"

"No, of course not," Brandy said. "Why would they want to do that?"

Instead of answering the question, Eve asked another. "Were all of your trucks in service on Wednesday and Thursday?"

"Yes, they were," she said.

"There weren't any in the shop or sidelined for any reason?"

"Nope," she said.

"Is your parking lot under video surveillance?"

"Twenty-four seven because of vandalism and people trying to steal tools and parts off the trucks," she said. "It's all recorded on DVR that recycles every sixty days."

"Thanks for your help, I appreciate it." Eve disconnected the call and saw Nan studying her.

"You're wondering how he got the bodies out of the house if he didn't use his car or his plumbing truck," Nan said.

The answer was obvious. "He had another car or an accomplice."

"Or both," Nan said.

The notion of a second killer had never occurred to Eve until now. Her entire focus for the last forty-eight-plus hours was finding a single individual. She didn't know where to start looking for a second man or woman.

"Is there any evidence you've seen that points to a second person?" Eve asked.

Nan shrugged. "Sometimes it's the lack of evidence that does the pointing."

Like it did right now, though Eve wasn't

convinced that a second person was the missing piece, not that she had the slightest idea what the hell it was. There was just a big, gaping hole in the case.

Eve felt a tremble of panic in her chest for the first time since the investigation began. It was the fear of failure and what it would mean. Her promotion to homicide detective would be condemned as a disastrous and irresponsible publicity stunt, one that revealed her arrogance and incompetence and the sheriff's frantic desperation to distract attention from the department's scandals. Their careers would be over and their reputations irreparably destroyed. They would deserve it, too.

But the prospect of that shame and ridicule wasn't what scared her the most. It was failing to get justice for Tanya, Caitlin, and Troy. She could not, she *would* not, let that happen.

# CHAPTER
# TWENTY-SEVEN

Calabasas was divided by steep hills that were designated as permanent open space. There were no roads that cut straight across them. As a result, to get to the other side of the city, it was necessary to take one of three routes: the 101 freeway to the north, the most direct route, but one that was often clogged with traffic, turning a three-mile drive into a thirty-minute ordeal; or Mulholland Highway, a two-lane road that took a long, winding route up and through the hills but required you to go several miles south and then backtrack north again; or a zigzag route that paralleled the freeway and crossed over it twice, following the crazy borders of a city created by piecemeal annexations of unincorporated land rather than a rational plan.

Eve took the zigzag route back to the Lost Hills station. That meant driving west on Calabasas Road, then north over the freeway to Mureau Road, a very narrow tree-lined street of deep dips, sudden rises, and sharp blind curves that inexplicably enticed people into speeding and led to frequent, and horrific, car accidents. But today there was so much traffic on the road, with frustrated commuters using it as an alternative to the clogged freeway, that speeding wasn't an option.

She hit the T intersection with Las Virgenes Road. Turning right would have taken her to the front door of her condo. Instead, she turned left and headed south over the freeway again, following the route she took to work most mornings on her bike.

She made a right onto Agoura Road and was passing the Good Nite Inn when guilt and responsibility tugged her into making a sharp U-turn and pulling into the hotel's parking lot. Cleve had told her during their encounter outside the Lost Hills station that this was where he'd be staying until the case was closed.

The Good Nite Inn was a two-star, two-story hotel with a low two-figure nightly rate, which brought the kind of clientele that guaranteed that sheriff's deputies visited often. The hotel had outdoor hallways and was buffeted by the sound of traffic rushing past from the freeway on one side and Agoura Road on the other. The exhaust fumes settled in the hotel's inner courtyard and mixed with the scent of the heavily chlorinated pool to create a toxic fragrance that kept the mosquitos away and probably killed bedbugs, too.

Eve called Cleve on the phone from her car and asked if she could see him. He told her to come on up and stood waiting for her in the open doorway of his second-floor room as she came up the stairs.

He was haggard, his hair askew, his eyes bloodshot, and he wore the wrinkled clothes from the previous night. His skin was pale, as if he'd been bled dry. Over his shoulder, Eve saw an unmade bed and a pizza box from Domino's and a liter bottle of Coca-Cola on the floor.

"Have you found my kids?" he asked, his voice low and hoarse. He stepped out of his doorway and went to the railing, making it clear he didn't want to have this conversation inside his room.

"No, but we've arrested a suspect and searched his home. We found this." She held up her phone to show Cleve a picture of the pink camera. "Can you tell me what this is?"

Cleve nodded, his chin trembling. "It's Caitlin's camera. I gave it to her as a birthday present a year ago."

"We found some pictures on it. Can you tell me when and where they were taken?"

She handed him the phone and let him scroll through Caitlin's pictures. All the shots were from a picnic at a lake with her brother, her father, and a golden retriever. There was only one picture of Caitlin, the one with the wet dog shaking off beside her. Caitlin was laughing and turning away, holding her hands up in a futile attempt to protect herself from getting wet but loving it all the same. It was a picture of pure happiness.

Now it was a picture that brought heartbreak. She thought he would have cried if he had any tears left. Instead, his body shook with emotional dry-heaves.

"Caitlin took these pictures in August at Lake Yosemite. It's a park up in Merced."

"Did she ever tell you that she'd lost the camera?"

He shook his head. "She might have told her mother but Caitlin wouldn't have said anything to me. She would have been worried about me being hurt or upset that she'd lost her birthday present." He handed the camera back to her, his hand shaking. "Who did you arrest?"

"His name is Lionel Coyle. He's a plumber who did some work at Tanya's house."

"What did you arrest him for?"

"Murder," Eve said, the word catching in her throat.

Cleve nodded, went back into his room, and closed the door softly behind him.

# CHAPTER
# TWENTY-EIGHT

Eve left the Good Nite Inn and drove the two blocks west to the Lost Hills station. The public parking lot was filled with satellite news trucks from the local TV channels. News of Coyle's arrest must have leaked. She drove past the trucks, through the gate, and into the lot reserved for official vehicles.

She went into the building, went straight to the squad room, and saw that Biddle and Garvey were at their desks and on their phones. They both acknowledged her with a nod. Duncan was at his desk, too, working his way through a mountain of paperwork. He looked up at her as she passed.

"Make any progress?" he asked.

"Two steps forward and one step back," she said.

"Let's hear about the steps forward."

"Coyle's got a drawer full of little knickknacks, stuff he could fit in his pocket, that he stole from the places he serviced as a plumber," she said and told him about cross-referencing Coyle's service calls with reports of crimes and how that led her to Vickie Denhoff and Esther Sondel. "I think he slipped into their houses later, when nobody was home, and took the items as souvenirs of his secret visit."

"How much of that can you prove?"

"The women picked out their stuff from photos of his collection and Cleve Kenworth ID'd the pink camera as Caitlin's." "How do you know he didn't steal those items during his service calls?" Duncan said. "It doesn't prove he broke into the house later or killed Tanya and her kids."

"There's more," she said. "Denhoff came home early from work one day and was raped by a guy wearing a monster mask who was hiding in her bedroom. I think Tanya walked in on him in her house."

"Did we get any DNA from Denhoff's rapist?"

Eve shook her head. "She cleaned herself up before reporting the rape."

"Is that the step back?"

"No, it's bigger than that," she said. "CSU hasn't found anything in Coyle's house or in his car that ties him to the murders. And before you ask, I checked with Mr. Plunger. All of their trucks were accounted for on Wednesday and Thursday, so he didn't use one of their vehicles."

Duncan frowned, but he didn't seem to Eve to be thrown by the setback, at least not to the degree that she was.

"Coyle could have borrowed or stolen a car," Duncan said. "Maybe one that belongs to one of his neighbors or a friend who was out of town."

"Even if he took another car to Tanya's house, we know he went back there again in his own car after he went to Walmart for supplies."

"Maybe he'd finished covering up his tracks as best he could in Tanya's house, hauled away the trash, and dumped the bodies and was going back to mop up the garage," Duncan said. "The floor in there is painted concrete, not blood-soaked carpet. If he was careful, he might have been able to do it without stepping in anything that he'd track back into his own car. Even if he did step in something, maybe he dropped his shoes into a trash bag and changed into another pair before getting back in his car."

Eve liked that theory because it ruled out a second person but it raised almost as many questions as it answered. "But why would he use two different cars to begin with?"

Duncan shrugged. "Why does he dress up as an ape?"

"Where did he go to clean himself up after he left Tanya's house and before he went to Walmart for more supplies to clean up the garage?"

"The same place where he got the other car, the out-of-town neighbor or friend," Duncan said. "He could have broken into their place or maybe he has a key and is collecting their mail or walking their dog while they are away. I can have Biddle and Garvey canvas the mobile home park, see if anybody knows something."

"That's a good idea," Eve said, feeling a lot better about the case than she did when she left Nan at Coyle's place, and it was thanks to Duncan. He saw a pothole where she saw a bottomless abyss. Then again, he didn't have as much riding on the case as she did. He had nothing to fear. It gave him the peace of mind to see the case from another perspective. She would remember that lesson.

"What's your next move?" he asked.

"I'll have a talk with Coyle and see what I can bluff out of him now," she said. "Unless you have a better idea."

"I wish I did," he said.

Eve went to her desk, printed out some photos, filled a file folder with a bunch of papers as a prop, picked up a yellow legal pad and pen, then went down the hall to the interrogation room.

Coyle was already inside and had been for twenty minutes. He slouched in his purposely wobbly chair. He was wearing blue jailhouse scrubs and his hands weren't cuffed.

Eve dumped the thick folder and notepad on the table and dropped into the stable chair across from him with a weary sigh.

"I'm absolutely exhausted. I would have come to talk to you sooner but we have been so busy." Eve patted the thick folder and shook her head. "I've never seen a case come together this quickly. Every time I was about to see you, more evidence and answers would come in. It finally slowed down a bit."

He stared at her but didn't say a word. She leaned toward him, resting her arms on the table.

"I'm not here to question you, Coyle, because we know everything."

"There's nothing to know," he said.

"Your drawer of souvenirs from the houses you broke into was a big help to us. I almost came by your cell to thank you. We would have discovered the woman you raped in West Hills when we ran your DNA through the system, but because you kept her tiny teacup, we found her today. She even recognized your monkey mask."

Coyle tried to keep a blank face but there was an involuntary twitch in his left eyelid that gave away that she'd scored a hit. Eve kept going.

"You left some DNA at Tanya's house and on the hill where you clobbered me, too. I won't bore you with all the evidence."

Coyle stared at her. "Then why are you here?"

Eve noted that he didn't deny what she said. That, in itself, felt like a confession to her, but it wasn't one. She needed more—much more.

"Because, between you and me, I'm the one homicide detective in the LASD who does not support the death penalty. We devote ourselves to catching killers, so how can we kill them in cold blood and call it justice? The thing is, what you did was so horrible, and the evidence is so overwhelming, that the jury will find you guilty after thirty seconds, tops, of deliberation and then they will sentence you to the needle. No question about it. But there's one thing right now I can do to change that outcome and that you can do to save yourself."

He seemed to sink deeper into his seat. It wobbled from side to side. "What's that?"

"I can get the DA to take the death penalty off the table if you tell me where they are."

"Who?"

Eve shook her head, like she was disappointed in him. "Come on, Coyle. I'm trying to do you a favor here. Tell me where to find Tanya, Caitlin, and Troy's body parts and you'll live."

His whole body language changed. He sat up straight and smiled. It was like seeing a puppet being lifted up by his strings and start to perform. She knew in that instant that she'd somehow overplayed her hand. He leaned forward and looked her in the eye with smug satisfaction.

"We're done talking," he said. "I want to call my lawyer."

# CHAPTER TWENTY-NINE

Eve walked out of the interrogation room, the file and notepad under her arm, and didn't let her anger show until the door was closed behind her. She'd tried to play him and somehow got played herself.

The door to the observation room opened and Duncan emerged with a woman carrying a briefcase. Eve didn't recognize her.

The woman said to Eve: "Don't be too hard on yourself, Detective. It was worth a try. But the bodies are like those souvenirs you found. He doesn't want to give them up. As long as we don't have them, he still does."

Duncan tipped his head toward the woman. "Do you know ADA Rebecca Burnside?"

Burnside had a grim, serious demeanor that Eve suspected the prosecutor worked hard to maintain to dim the wattage of her fashion-model beauty. But her looks were something Burnside curated with care, putting time into applying her makeup, styling her shoulder-length hair, and choosing suits that accentuated her figure without exploiting it.

Eve offered Burnside her hand. "I appreciate your fast work on those warrants."

They shook hands. Burnside's grip was as firm as a linebacker's. "My pleasure. Let's go to the conference room and you can tell me what we really have on him and what is fake news."

Eve led them down the hall and into the conference room, which was filled by a long table with ten chairs, four on each side and one on each end. The blinds were drawn on the window, which looked out over the back parking lot.

Burnside took a seat at one end and the two detectives each took a seat on either side of her. She pulled a legal pad out of her briefcase, set it in front of her, and uncapped a Mont Blanc pen. "Let's start with your theory of the case."

"Lionel Coyle is a plumber who does service calls for insurance companies," Eve said. "He goes back to the houses, particularly the ones occupied by women, when they are empty. He dresses up, at least partially, as an ape and roams around the empty home, searching for something small and personal he can steal as a souvenir that won't be immediately missed. Then something changed."

"A woman walked in on him in West Hills," Duncan said. "And he raped her."

"You think he liked it and that inspired him to change his MO," Burnside said.

"That's right," Eve said. "I believe he watched Tanya's house from the hillside behind it and learned her routine. Once he was sure the house was empty, he broke in and waited for her to come home so he could rape her. Something went wrong and the rape became a murder. Things escalated from there and one murder became three, not counting the dog."

Burnside made some notes and doodled around some of the words. "And in the middle of all this, you think he made a run to Walmart to get more supplies."

"We think he ditched the bodies and cleaned himself up first," Eve said. "But yes, he went out to Walmart, went back to the house to do some last-minute cleanup, then left again."

"But you believe he came back to the scene of the crime the next morning," Burnside said. "When you were already on scene."

"That's right," Eve said. "He parked his car at the Topanga State Park trailhead down the street, hiked through the park to the hill above Tanya's house, and retrieved his sleeping bag and some other trash that he'd left behind when he was staking out the place."

Burnside made some more doodles, giving some of the words a 3-D effect and sketching a movie marque around them. "It was the plastic bag in the garage that led you to Walmart and to a suspect. You saw him on surveillance video leave the Walmart in a Toyota Corolla, which you matched to the license plate of a Corolla at the Topanga Park trailhead, which is how you identified Coyle. You obtained a search warrant on his home and car, which you served this morning. Based on what you saw during that initial search, you arrested him for murder."

"That's correct," Eve said.

Burnside leaned back in her chair. "What did you see that prompted you to arrest him?"

"We found Caitlin's camera, with photos of her and her brother on the memory card, in his home and an earring that may belong to her mother," Eve said. "We also found a pair of shoes that match those worn by the killer."

"But not the actual shoes," Burnside said.

"No," Eve said.

"We did find an ape suit," Duncan said. "He could have been wearing that mask when he raped the lady in West Hills."

Once again, Eve felt the guilt and shame of what her pride had cost her. If she'd told Duncan about being attacked by a "monster" at the crime scene, the ape suit could have been compelling evidence against Coyle. But she didn't tell anyone, so now it was worthless. It was a huge mistake, one she'd carry for the rest of her life if Coyle got away with the murders.

"Did the victim really identify the ape mask?" Burnside asked and Eve shook her head. "And we don't actually have any DNA evidence, do we?"

Burnside drilled her with a gaze and Eve knew the ADA wanted to hear an answer this time.

"No," Eve said.

"You're saying that he raped that woman but all we actually have is a miniature teacup," Burnside said. "I haven't researched this yet, but I don't think in the history of criminal law that a miniature teacup has ever led to a rape conviction."

"He did it," Eve said, angered by Burnside's contempt and even more so by her belief that she probably deserved it. "Coyle was rattled when I brought up the rape."

"I'd be rattled by a false rape accusation, too," Burnside said.

"It wasn't," Eve said. "He's a rapist and he's a killer."

Burnside didn't argue the point. "Okay, let's get back to the killing. Is there any other evidence that's been found in his mobile home or car that ties him to the murders?"

Duncan spoke up, clearly trying to take some of the pressure off Eve: "The camera and the earring put him in Tanya's house."

"Wasn't he in her house before the murders fixing their toilet or something?" Burnside asked.

"Coyle was sent to her house twice by Mr. Plunger," Duncan said. "That's when he stole a spare key or unlocked a window so he could slip in later."

"How do we know he didn't steal the camera and the earring during those two prior visits?" Burnside asked.

"We don't," Eve said, sparing Duncan from being the target of Burnside's contempt.

"So even if we get lucky and find his DNA in the house, it's worthless," Burnside said. "His lawyer will simply argue it was left during those previous visits."

There was a knock on the door. Before Eve could get up to answer it, the door swung open and Captain Moffett came in, followed by Sheriff Richard Lansing.

The sheriff glanced at their faces.

"I was expecting a celebration," he said. "So why does it look like I just walked in on a funeral?"

# CHAPTER THIRTY

Moffett and Lansing were both in uniform, as if they were actually prepared to hit the streets for patrol duty, something neither one of them had done in years. Eve, Duncan, and Burnside immediately stood up when they saw the sheriff.

Lansing was in his late fifties, square-jawed, square-shouldered, and socially square, the son of a preacher and currently a man besieged, facing a beating scandal at the county jail that seemed to be getting worse every day. Now that he was here, Eve understood who tipped off the media and why, and it made her uncomfortable. He wanted to announce a big arrest to take some of the pressure off himself, even if it was far too soon to do so.

"Please sit down, everyone. The captain informed me of the arrest in the Topanga Massacre," Lansing said, closing the door behind him. Eve wasn't aware the case now had a title, and a lurid one at that. "Where do we stand with Coyle?"

"On thin ice," Burnside said.

Eve felt her face flush with anger. Burnside's blunt assessment riled her but, at the same time, she could see the truth behind it. Eve knew with complete certainty Coyle was the killer even if there wasn't yet enough evidence to prove it in a courtroom.

"How do you figure that?" Lansing said, taking a seat at the other end of the table. "From what I've heard from the captain, we've got a shitload of evidence."

Moffett sat to one side of the sheriff and looked down the long table at Burnside at the far end.

"*Shitload* is the right word," Burnside said. "It's entirely circumstantial and there are big holes in the narrative. We can prove he was in the house, but not on the day of the murder. A good lawyer will tear us apart with that. The only case I could make in court today is for burglary."

"Then it's fortunate we aren't in court today, isn't it?" Lansing said. "I believe you are mistaken, Counselor. We have a strong case that's only going to get stronger as more evidence is gathered and analyzed. We have momentum on our side."

"I agree," Captain Moffett said.

*Of course he did,* Eve thought. Both men badly needed a win, something positive to tell the media that would redirect the spotlight away from their scandals and failures. Burnside pissed Eve off, but she admired the ADA for her integrity. Burnside wasn't afraid to stand up to the sheriff.

"Look what the task force has accomplished already," Lansing said. "It's phenomenal. The important thing now is finding the bodies. Everything else will fall into place after that."

Lansing shifted his gaze to Eve. "You took a butcher off the streets in record time. I'm damn impressed."

"It was a team effort, sir," Eve said.

"Bullshit. You made the key discoveries that led us to Coyle. Own it. You have the right stuff, Ronin. The public saw it in that YouTube video and so did I. That's why I granted your transfer to RHD, and not to capitalize on your publicity, as some people thought." Lansing glanced sharply at Moffett, then back to Eve. "I'm having a press conference out front in ten minutes. I want you, Burnside, and the captain there with me."

Eve wasn't surprised about the immediate press conference, but she was struck by his blatant hypocrisy. He'd just denied that he was motivated by publicity when he promoted her and then, in the next breath with a straight face, he'd said he wanted her at a press conference. It was duplicity born out of his desperate political need, now and then, to capitalize on the good news and distract the public from the scandals in the department.

But there were dozens of reasons why Eve thought it was a bad idea for the department and the case if they stepped in front of the cameras now. For one thing, Burnside was right. Come Monday, the judge could see that all they had was a burglary case and let Coyle walk out on bail— then they'd all be humiliated.

"I think it's too soon to be holding a press

conference," she said. "We shouldn't go public until we have more evidence."

Moffett and Burnside stared at her in shock. Duncan simply grimaced. Some color rose in Lansing's cheeks. He glared at her.

"Are you telling me you have doubts about your case?"

"I'm certain that he's the killer," Eve said.

"Then I expect to see you express that certainty to those reporters." Lansing got to his feet. "Don't put on any makeup. It's important that they see how hard working and tired you are."

*Mom will love that,* Eve thought. Lansing walked out and Moffett joined him.

Eve looked at Burnside. "You know I'm right."

"I already expressed my opinion and he rejected it," Burnside said.

Duncan nodded in agreement and looked at Eve. "You should have taken the hint."

"I couldn't just stand by and say nothing," Eve said.

"Yes," Duncan said. "We noticed."

Burnside stuffed her legal pad into her briefcase and stood up. "The fact is that we have a suspect in custody. The public will be glad to hear it. That's a win. This press conference will make you a star again."

"I don't want the spotlight."

"But we do." Burnside smiled at her and walked out.

Eve revised her opinion of Burnside's integrity. The integrity was there, but it had limitations. It was trumped by her ambition. Burnside was willing to gamble that enjoying the glory today wouldn't lead to shame next week. It was a raw political calculation and Burnside was probably making a smart bet. If Lansing, Moffett, and Eve went down, Burnside could still come out relatively unscathed, saying she was given a bad case.

Eve met Duncan's eye. "I'm fucked."

"Not if you can prove Coyle did it," Duncan said. "How hard could that be?"

# CHAPTER
# THIRTY-ONE

The front steps of the Lost Hills station had become a stage. Lansing stood at a wooden podium with a Los Angeles County Sheriff's Department seal on the front and faced the lights of a dozen TV cameras and two dozen print and broadcast reporters. Captain Moffett, ADA Burnside, and Eve stood in the background. Eve wondered where the podium came from, if it was kept in a closet somewhere in the station or if Lansing carried it around in his Ford Expedition.

"Based on the evidence recovered at the crime scene and the tireless work of our detectives, under the supervision of Captain Moffett, we're now certain that Tanya Kenworth and her two children, Caitlin and Troy, were brutally murdered in their Topanga Canyon home on Wednesday," Lansing said. "This is the tragic, heartbreaking outcome that we all feared."

He paused, letting the horrible news sink in, but Eve saw it as a cheap ploy to jack up the drama of the moment. She also had the heart-sinking realization that in their rush to the cameras, nobody had bothered to call Cleve first before they told the world his kids were slaughtered. It was one more cruel, insensitive oversight she'd have to add to her list of regrets in this case.

When the sheriff spoke again, there was anger and determination on his face, and his right hand was balled into a fist.

"But justice will prevail. I can promise you that." Lansing hammered his fist on the podium. "Because we have a suspect in custody. His name is Lionel Coyle, a man that Assistant District Attorney Burnside will be prosecuting to the fullest extent of the law."

That revelation caused an instant commotion among the press. The reporters all started to fire off questions at once, but Kate Darrow's voice rose above the others.

"What is the suspect's relation to the family?"

"He's a plumber who did some work at the house," Lansing said.

His response prompted a flurry of other questions, only a few of which Eve was able to hear.

"Why did he kill them?"

"Was the boyfriend or the ex-husband involved?"

"Was he a member of a cult?"

"How were they killed?"

"Have you recovered the murder weapon?"

Lansing held up his hands in a halting gesture to silence the questions and continue with his statement.

"The quick capture of the monster responsible for this heinous crime is due, in large measure, to the exceptional investigative work of Eve Ronin, the youngest Robbery-Homicide detective in the history of the Los Angeles County Sheriff's Department."

He turned and waved her up to the podium. Eve stepped forward, mentally visualizing the notes she'd made on her legal pad, and faced the sheriff before addressing the press.

"Thank you, sir, but I'm just one of many detectives working on this case and don't deserve the credit." Eve now turned in the general direction of the cameras, the glare of the lights making it impossible to see the faces of the reporters or the lenses. "We are all deeply saddened and horrified by this senseless crime. Our hearts go out to the family and loved ones of Tanya, Caitlin, and Troy Kenworth. We won't stop until their bodies are recovered and laid properly to rest."

"You said 'senseless,' " Kate Darrow said. "Does that mean you have no motive for this crime?"

Before Eve could answer, Lansing quickly stepped up to the podium and gently, but firmly, shouldered her aside.

"We'll be giving you photos of Mr. Coyle and his Toyota Corolla to share with your audience. We are very interested in his movements on

Wednesday and Thursday of last week. If you saw him, please call our tip line. You can leave your information anonymously. That's all for tonight. We won't be taking any further questions at this time."

Lansing led Eve, Moffett, and Burnside back into the station as reporters fired off a barrage of questions at their backs.

"I don't want any of you talking to the press," Lansing said to the three of them in the lobby. "From now on, any contact with the media will go through our media affairs office."

That was an order for Eve and Moffett, but Burnside answered to a different authority, the district attorney, who might want to hold a press conference of his own but probably wouldn't rush until he saw how Monday's arraignment played out.

Eve was headed for the squad room but Lansing called after her.

"Ronin," Lansing said. "Could I have a word?"

He drew her aside to a corner of the lobby, by a wall of framed eight-by-tens of the sheriff, the captain, and various command personnel. They reminded Eve of the signed headshots from celebrities on the walls of dry cleaners, restaurants, car repair shops, and other businesses throughout Los Angeles.

She knew what this little talk was going to be about and decided to take the initiative. "I'm sorry, sir. I should never have said 'senseless.' I should have chosen my words more carefully."

He waved away her concern. "You did good. The camera loves you."

"My mother would disagree with you, but thanks." Eve started to turn away. "I've got a lot of work to do."

"Hold on. You've caught the killer, that was the hard part. The pressure is off," Lansing said.

"We still need to gather a lot more evidence to secure a murder conviction," Eve said.

"You'll get it, but now every move you make is going to be under the media spotlight. Delegate the rest of the work tonight to the detectives who are outside of that glare. I want you to go home and get some rest."

"Thank you, but the arraignment is on Monday and I want—"

He interrupted her. "You aren't hearing me. If you look tired and haggard tomorrow, after you've already caught the killer, the press is going to wonder why you are working so Goddamn hard. They will think our case is weak. But if you look bright, refreshed, and relaxed the next time they see you, that projects confidence, and that's what they will feel about the case, too." Lansing tipped his head to the press outside, many of them still on camera, using the station as a backdrop for their reporting on the story.

"The press isn't following me around all the time."

"Today everybody has a camera. You, of all people, should know that. Perception is reality, so it's up to us to create the perception," Lansing said. There was a contradiction in that last statement but she wasn't entirely sure it was unintentional. "I think you're going to have a bright future in this department."

*Not if this case falls apart,* she thought.

"Go home," Lansing said. "That's an order."

# CHAPTER
# THIRTY-TWO

Eve got a deputy to give her a ride back to her condo. She ran inside, grabbed the keys to her Subaru Outback, and drove to Barnes & Noble at the Commons in Calabasas, where she bought a large map of the San Fernando Valley. From there, she went to the Office Depot on Topanga to buy a box of colored pushpins and then went two blocks south to Yang Chow, a Chinese restaurant across from the Topanga Mall, and bought fried rice, Slippery Shrimp, and chow mein to go. She took her purchases home, devoured her dinner, and got to work.

Back when she was a detective in burglary, she got a lot of results using geographic profiling. The basic idea behind it is that people commit crimes close to where they live, work, and play because it's easier to find prey, and make a quick escape, in areas they know well.

She knew that geographic profiling worked best as a technique to pinpoint the home or workplace of criminals committing serial crimes. She'd nailed several serial burglars by marking the location of each burglary on a map, drawing a radius of three miles around each scene, and focusing her attention on where the circles overlapped. It inevitably led her to where the crook lived or worked or to where he'd strike next.

Now she figured it would work in reverse, helping her determine where Coyle had most likely dumped the bodies. Eve only had three confirmed locations where Coyle committed crimes, but she knew he used his service calls as scouting trips for burglaries. So she decided to treat each service call as a possible crime scene and plot them all on a map of the San Fernando Valley. There was a crucial flaw in her approach—since Coyle was assigned his calls, he didn't choose them. But she decided to see if a pattern emerged that might suggest there were some areas he spent more time in than others and would feel more comfortable going back to for his burglaries . . . or to dump bags of body parts.

It would be easier for the Crime Analysis Unit to pinpoint the hot zones for her, utilizing a profiling algorithm specifically designed for geographic profiling, but she liked the tactile effort of doing it herself and she believed that might give her a better intuitive understanding of Coyle's movements. Besides, what else did she have to do tonight?

So Eve put the map of the valley up on her living room wall and marked the locations of the Mr. Plunger office, Coyle's home, Tanya's home,

Vickie Denhoff's house, and Esther Sondel's house on it with a Sharpie.

She then used colored pushpins to start marking the location of every service call Coyle had made. There were hundreds, but she hoped a cluster or pattern would emerge before she had nine hundred pins in the map.

A few hours later, she had several hundred pins on the map, and was beginning to see the densest number of calls were in Calabasas, Topanga, and Malibu, when her iPhone rang. She found the phone under the Mr. Plunger printouts and glanced at the screen. It was her mom calling. Her first instinct was to dismiss the call but for reasons she would never understand, she answered it.

"Hey, Mom. Let me guess. You saw the press conference."

"It was your best performance yet."

"It wasn't a performance," Eve said.

"You came across as a confident, capable detective."

"I like to think that's because I am," Eve said.

"You were racked with self-doubt and insecurity."

"No, I wasn't," Eve said, plucking cold chow mein noodles from the still-open container and eating them. "What makes you say that?"

"When Kate Darrow nailed you with that 'senseless' question, you looked away. When you're sure of yourself, you like to stare people down. Trust me, I've seen that stare enough to know."

Eve was embarrassed that she had such an obvious tell and wondered if that was what Coyle had spotted in the interrogation room.

"It was the glare of TV lights," Eve said. "They were hurting my eyes."

"You don't lie enough to be good at it, honey. You've got problems with your case but don't worry, it's not going to hurt the chances of you becoming a TV movie."

"That's not something I care about."

"You will if you get fired. It will be found money."

"Thanks for the vote of confidence," Eve said.

"You could learn a few things from Rebecca Burnside about wardrobe and makeup. Why can't you dress like her?"

"Because I work on the street and she works in a courtroom, which is a lot like being on stage. The audience she plays to is the judge and jury. Doing a press conference is just an extension of that performance. She's facing potential jurors. I've got to dress for what I do. I can't chase bad guys in high heels."

"I'm impressed," Jen said. "You pretend that you aren't playing to an audience but you are. Now I get it. You've *chosen* to dress the way you do, and to ignore your hair and makeup, because you're creating a distinct character."

"I'm not creating anything. It's who I am, Mom."

"You mean you're consistently staying in character. Very sharp. I'm not sure I agree with your creative choices, but I admire what you're doing. You're more like me than you think."

"You're reading me all wrong," Eve said, but without much of a fight behind it. Her mother had made a very convincing argument. What if she was right? It was too disturbing to contemplate.

"I love you, hardnose." Jen made a kissing sound into the phone. "Get some sleep."

"I will," Eve said, but she didn't go to bed.

She spent another hour putting pins in the map and then, after accidentally sticking herself in the finger with a pushpin, she decided to take a break and approach her investigation from another angle.

Eve opened up her laptop on the coffee table, logged on to Amazon, and rented the original *Planet of the Apes*, hoping it might give her some insights into Coyle. She sat back on the couch and watched as astronaut Charlton Heston crashed on an alien planet where apes were the superior species and humans were inferior.

It was a heavy-handed allegorical tale, and although the apes were more advanced than man, they didn't have any technology and lived in earthen huts in a time period similar to the Old West.

She fell asleep and dreamed of apes on horseback rampaging through the women's department of Neiman Marcus.

# CHAPTER THIRTY-THREE

The sound of the doorbell ringing, and a fist pounding on the door, woke Eve up, dazed and disoriented.

"Hold on, Mom, I'm coming." Eve got up from the couch, stretched her stiff back, and shuffled to the door. But it wasn't her mom standing outside, it was Duncan Pavone holding a box of donuts, a sight that Eve found very confusing, since she'd just been talking to her mom on the phone.

She looked at her hand and realized she wasn't holding a phone and hadn't been talking to anyone. The fog in her head began to clear. Her mom had been banging on the door *yesterday*. This was a new day, a new rude awakening.

"Sorry to make such a racket, but you didn't answer the phone." Duncan invited himself in and gave her the once-over as she closed the door. "Isn't that what you wore yesterday?"

Eve went back to the couch to look for her phone. "What's the big emergency?"

"Coyle's lawyer called. They want to talk to us."

She found her phone on the coffee table. The phone's battery was dead. "What do they want to talk about?"

"Maybe he wants to confess. Or maybe he still wants that selfie with you." Duncan went to the map on the wall, which was covered with pushpins. "What is this?"

"All of Coyle's service calls. The Xs mark Coyle's house, Tanya's house, and where he works. I'm trying to use geographical profiling to figure out where the bodies may be. It's where Coyle goes when he's not breaking into houses, raping, and killing people that will be the key to finding the bodies." She pointed to the circles she'd drawn in a three-mile radius from Tanya's house, Esther Sondel's house, and some of the other service calls. "The rape in West Hills was an outlier. I think we'll find the bodies on one of these clusters of pins where the circles overlap."

Most of those pushpins marking service calls were grouped in the southeastern edge of Calabasas and the Santa Monica Mountains near Topanga Canyon to the east and Las Virgenes to the west.

Eve picked up her shoes and socks, sat on the arm of the couch, and put them on.

Duncan looked at the map, then at the papers strewn amid the Chinese takeout boxes, and shook his head. "I've seen TV cops do this, but never a real person."

"Do what?"

"Bring a case home and put it on their wall

to illustrate their obsession. Is that where you picked this up? A TV show?"

"The sheriff ordered me to go home but I still had work to do, that's all." She went to the kitchen, opened the refrigerator, and took out a can of Coke.

"You caught the bad guy. You were publicly commended by the sheriff. You've already proven yourself. You can stop trying so hard to impress everybody."

Eve popped open the can, took a mouthful of Coke, swished it around, and spit it out like mouthwash. "That's not what I'm doing."

"Well, not right now," he said, then gestured to the wall. "All of this work isn't impressive. It's kind of pathetic."

She took another swig of Coke, but this time she swallowed it. "I just want to close the case. There are big holes we need to fill or tomorrow morning Coyle could be back on the street."

Duncan sighed. "I've been doing this for decades. I've solved lots of crimes. I've put away some very bad people. I'm a damn good detective, if I do say so myself."

"I know you are." Eve had some more Coke and wondered where he was going with this.

"But now that my career is nearly over, do you want to know what I am most proud of? Being married for thirty years and raising two kids who don't hate me. I'm not an alcoholic or a prescription drug addict, either. All of that makes me an exception to the rule in our profession."

She tilted her can of Coke toward the box of donuts in his hands. "You eat a ton of donuts."

"Because it makes me happy," he said. "I made happiness a priority. That's key to achieving my stats."

Eve set her empty can on the table and gathered up her badge and gun. "I can't be happy when things are unsettled. Order is what makes me happy."

"You can't keep up like this, Eve. You'll burn out fast."

She pocketed her badge and holstered her gun on her belt. She was ready to go. "It's just this one case."

"Uh-huh," Duncan said. "You aren't going to change your clothes?"

Eve lifted her arms and sniffed under her armpits. "I'm good."

Duncan handed her the box of donuts. "I'll drive while you have breakfast."

# CHAPTER
# THIRTY-FOUR

It was 8:40 on Sunday morning. The Santa Ana winds were blowing at thirty miles an hour through the Los Angeles Basin, fanning the flames in Valencia, and humidity was barely measurable, prompting the fourth straight day of red flag warnings in Los Angeles, Ventura, and Santa Barbara counties.

The ride to the Men's Central Jail in downtown Los Angeles, where Coyle had been transferred on the previous night, took them nearly ninety minutes in rush-hour traffic, though "rush hour" was a misnomer. The traffic ordinarily didn't ebb until about lunchtime, even on Sunday, and that was only if there were no serious accidents to clear.

The Men's Central Jail was the epicenter of the ongoing scandals that were dogging the department. Now that the jail was under a media and Justice Department spotlight, every deputy and civilian employee was on their best behavior, assuming that any prisoner, lawyer, or family member entering the facility was a potential media source or FBI informant.

Eve and Duncan locked up their weapons, filled out the necessary paperwork, and were led to an interview room where Coyle and his lawyer were already waiting. Coyle was relaxed, stretched out in his hard chair as if it were a comfy recliner. The lawyer stood up and introduced herself as Stella Winters. She was a short, barrel-bodied woman in her fifties whose chin seemed to have been absorbed by her neck. A man would have compensated for his lost chin by growing a beard to establish some definition. Winters tried to use makeup to create some shadow but it didn't work.

"Thank you for coming down, Detectives," Winters said. "We won't keep you long."

"Why isn't the assistant district attorney here?" Eve asked as she sat down.

"Because Burnside is not the one with the most at stake here," Winters said.

"Say what?" Duncan said. "Your client is the one looking at the death penalty. Are there stakes higher than death?"

Winters gave him a polite smile, the kind reserved for someone you don't want to hurt who has told a bad joke. "This case will never get that far, Detective Pavone. The only charge Mr. Coyle faces is petty theft of a digital camera and even that charge is weak."

Eve sighed. "We can prove he butchered a woman, two children, and their dog."

"You wish you could. You've found nothing at the crime scene, at his home, in his car, or on

239

his person that ties him to those murders. The fact is, all you can prove is that my client was in that family's house twice, at their request, to fix plumbing problems. That's a shameful basis for an arrest," Winters said. "We're giving you an opportunity today to redeem yourself before it's too late."

"You've got to be kidding me," Eve said.

Winters leaned across the table toward Eve, as if to confide in her. "You are the face of this investigation, Detective Ronin. You are the one who will be pilloried and ruined when I get this case thrown out due to an appalling lack of sufficient evidence. But if you drop the charges now, there's a chance your career might survive the justified humiliation. You can blame your youth, inexperience, and overzealousness. You can blame the sheriff for exploiting your YouTube popularity as a salve for his scandals. Mr. Coyle might even be willing to publicly forgive you."

Coyle smiled and winked at Eve. "Only if I can have that selfie with you."

Eve knew the lawyer was right about what would happen to her if the case against Coyle cratered on Monday. But Winters overestimated how important Eve's career was to her and how much she was willing to sacrifice for it. Eve was far more afraid of living with the guilt of letting a killer go free than she was about being humiliated and losing her job. She didn't deserve to have the badge if she couldn't keep Coyle in a cell.

"I have a better idea, Lionel," Eve said. "You can tell us where to find the bodies and we'll take the death penalty off the table."

Coyle dropped his gaze to her chest. "You have sprinkles on your shirt."

Eve looked down and, sure enough, there were some multicolored sugar sprinkles on her blouse from the donut she ate in the car. She wiped the sprinkles off, well aware that Coyle was using it as an excuse to stare at her breasts. It also meant she had his full attention and she was going to use it.

"I watched *Planet of the Apes* in bed last night." She added the "in bed" to tantalize him. It worked. His breath caught and he looked her in the eye.

"Did you like it?"

"It's cheesy fun, but I don't see why you're so wild about it."

"Because it's a great movie that works on so many levels. It really says something about our society and all of the things that are wrong with it."

Eve shook her head. "It's more than that to you, Lionel. You have an ape suit in your closet."

Winters spoke up. "Nice try, Detective, but my client is not going to answer any—"

Coyle interrupted her, his eyes still on Eve.

"You make it sound like having an ape suit is something crazy. It's no different than a *Star Trek* fan who has a Starfleet uniform."

"Who says that isn't crazy, too?" Duncan said.

But Coyle ignored Duncan. He was only interested in what Eve had to say.

"It's not just the one movie you like, it's all the sequels and spin-offs, too," Eve said. "What's the attraction?"

"It's a world upside down. It's a place where apes, creatures that we consider inferior today, are ruling the world and keeping humans as house pets, slaves, and lab animals."

"It sounds to me like you're rooting for the apes."

"I am."

"But aren't they the bad guys?"

Winters spoke up again, directing herself to Coyle this time. "Mr. Coyle, I must insist that you—"

"You're missing the point of the movie, Deathfist," Coyle said, speaking over Winters' objection. "The bad guys are whoever it is who think they are better than everybody else. This world needs to be turned upside down."

"I'll have to watch the movie again," Eve said. "Where's the DVD you bought at Walmart?"

That question made Coyle's eyelid twitch, just like it did when Eve told him yesterday that she'd tied him to Vickie Denhoff's rape. Eve found it very curious that mentioning the DVD got the same involuntary response.

Winters slapped her hand on the table. "This conversation is over. We're not here to answer your questions. We're making you a face-saving offer. You should take it. The offer expires in an hour."

"You heard Detective Ronin's generous offer," Duncan said. "I'd take it if I were you, Lionel. Because if we find the bodies without your help—"

Duncan jerked violently in his chair as if a thousand volts were coursing through his body.

Winters bolted up out of her seat in outrage. "That's enough! That was way out of line, Detective."

"She's right." Eve turned to Duncan and stood up, too. "You were wrong. They don't use the electric chair anymore. It's lethal injection."

"That's what lethal injection looks like." Duncan rose to his feet and smiled at Coyle. "When they screw up the dosage and the prisoner endures intense agony. You'll see."

Eve and Duncan walked out, closed the door, and headed down the corridor toward the iron security gate, which was manned by a guard. She was troubled by the encounter with Coyle. She couldn't get a sense of what he or his lawyer hoped to gain from it. Did they really think she'd drop the charges to save herself?

"That was a strange meeting," Eve said.

"He wants out of jail, that's all, and believes we don't have the evidence to hold him."

"So why not wait until tomorrow and have the pleasure of humiliating me and the entire department in court?" She had the nagging feeling that she was missing something important.

"He hates being cooped up and the more time he gives us, the better the odds are that we'll get the evidence we need but don't have yet. They had nothing to lose by taking the shot."

Eve didn't buy it. "If Stella Winters really believed we had nothing, she'd relish the opportunity to skin us alive in open court in front of the media. It would raise her public profile, bring her clients, maybe even get her a legal pundit gig on CNN. Something else is going on here."

"Not everybody looks at the media angle first and how they can leverage it for personal gain."

Eve ignored the swipe at her. They reached the security gate and were buzzed through by the guard on duty. They walked down another corridor toward the next gate.

"Where did Coyle find Winters?" Eve asked.

"He didn't. His mother did. Stella Winters represented Coyle on those jerking-off-in-public cases when he was in high school and at Pierce College. Winters got the charges dropped in exchange for him going into counseling."

"Winters must be good," Eve said. "How did Coyle's mother get so lucky?"

"Beatrice worked as a receptionist at a law firm in Woodland Hills and one of the lawyers there recommended Winters."

"What happened to Lionel's father?"

"I don't know. Beatrice was a single parent, never married," Duncan said. "Why did you ask Coyle about the DVD he bought at Walmart? Out of all the questions we have, that had to be the least important one."

"It made his eyelid twitch. I wonder why that is."

"Fatigue, dry eye, a nervous tick. Who cares? You wasted an opportunity on something insignificant."

"Is imitating death by electric chair an effective interrogation technique for you?"

"It doesn't get any answers," Duncan said, "but it never fails to amuse me."

# CHAPTER
# THIRTY-FIVE

Eve and Duncan walked into a squad room that was packed with detectives and deputies talking on telephones and taking notes. It reminded Eve of a telethon phone bank. Biddle and Garvey were at their side-by-side cubicles, doing paperwork.

"What are all these people doing here?" Eve asked Duncan.

"After the press conference last night, the tip lines lit up. The sheriff assigned a bunch of personnel to answer phones and more deputies to the search for the bodies. The captain is having the watch commander coordinate the search, which is expanding beyond the department to volunteer groups."

"We could make better use of some of those people who are answering phones," Eve said. "I'd like to see them out on the street, visiting each home Coyle serviced as a plumber and seeing if we can match more of his souvenirs to his past clients. Getting some more hits on Coyle's burglaries will help us use the geographic profile of his movements to narrow down the hot zones where the bodies might be buried."

"You're the task force leader," Duncan said.

"You can allocate the personnel any way you want."

"Okay, then let's do it. We still need to know a lot more about Coyle's life. The answer to what he did with the bodies may lie in what he's done in the past and what he likes to do when he isn't unclogging toilets or chopping up families. You and me and Crockett and Tubbs should talk to his coworkers, his neighbors, any relatives he might have. Am I missing anything?"

Duncan smiled at her. "Nope."

"Why are you smiling?"

"I like that you're confident but not over-confident," Duncan said. "Smart people are the ones who know how stupid they are."

"I'm not sure that tracks, or that it's a compliment, but I'll take it."

Garvey wheeled backward in his chair from his cubicle as he saw them approach. "How did it go with monkey boy?"

"It was a waste of time," Eve said, scanning all the pictures of Garvey with film, music, and sports celebrities that lined the three walls of his cubicle. There was one taken in the Lost Hills lobby with an intoxicated A-list movie star after he was released without being charged, no doubt thanks to Garvey's intervention.

Duncan flashed a sly grin. "I wouldn't say that."

Biddle shared a knowing look with Garvey,

then looked back at Duncan. "Did you do your electric chair shtick?"

"Hell yes," Duncan said and the three men laughed.

"Then it was time well spent," Biddle said. "That might have been your last chance to do it before your retirement party."

"He'll do it at the party," Garvey said. "You'll see."

Eve was impatient. She gestured to all the people on the phones. "Are we getting anything at all from the tip lines?"

"We've had over two hundred tips since last night's episode of *Deathfist and the Sheriff*," Garvey said. "One caller says he saw Coyle digging graves in Palmdale, another thinks he saw him in the desert near Palm Springs."

"A lady is sure she sat next to him on the Universal Studios tour and that he copped a feel," Biddle added.

"We're feeding any tips related to possible burial spots to the watch commander, who is coordinating the search parties," Garvey said. "But we're keeping a file of the tips that deserve a closer look from seasoned detectives."

"Show me the file," Eve said. Garvey handed her an empty file folder. "Really? We've got nothing?"

"Nothing even remotely useful has come in from the tip lines," Garvey said.

"It's almost always a waste of time and resources," Biddle said. "Though we usually get some good stories out of it to share at parties."

"Is there any good news?" Eve asked.

"Coyle was the guy who attacked you on the hill," Biddle said. "CSU got a DNA match off the piss they collected up there."

"Yee-haw," Garvey said. "We can't prove he's a murderer, but we've got him for petty theft and hitting Deathfist with a rock. Quick, schedule a press conference and break out the champagne."

It wasn't much progress, but Eve found it encouraging anyway. "Any other DNA hits?"

"Not yet," Biddle said.

At least he held out some hope, Eve thought. Her phone, which she'd recharged in Duncan's car, vibrated in her pocket to alert her to a text message. She took out the phone and checked the screen. It was a text from Nan. She read it and shared the message with her team.

"CSU has finished their work at the crime scene and are releasing the house to Jared Rawlins," Eve said and pocketed her phone. "I'm going out there. I'd like one more look at it before it goes public and gets trampled."

"You think Jared will open his house up for tours?" Duncan asked.

Eve vividly recalled the TV footage of reporters trooping through the Redlands condo that belonged to the husband-and-wife shooters behind the Inland Regional Center massacre in San Bernardino. The landlord opened the condo to a swarm of reporters and camera crews within minutes of the FBI releasing the property to him. There were still clothes hanging in the closets, food and baby formula in the refrigerator, papers scattered on desks, prescription bottles in the medicine cabinets, and dirty dishes in the sink, and all of it got pawed and photographed by the press.

"It's happened before," she said.

"We'll dig deep into Coyle's pathetic life in the meantime," Duncan said. "I'll call you if anything comes up."

# CHAPTER
# THIRTY-SIX

Eve had the house to herself. The CSU
investigators had removed the cones, tape, and
other evidence markers, as well as a few small
sections of carpet, drywall, and bathroom tile
for testing, but otherwise the crime scene hadn't
significantly changed since her last visit. The
overpowering smell of cleansers and motor oil
had either dissipated or she'd become nose-
blind to it. All she could hear was the thunderous
whoosh of the dry, hot Santa Anas blowing past
and the whistling that the winds created in the
chimney.

She stood in the kitchen, cleared her head,
and tried to imagine how the murders occurred,
letting the events play out as if they were
happening right in front of her . . .

Tanya rushed past Eve into the kitchen
for a quick bite before showering and
changing to meet her Realtor. She was
in her tank top and leggings, her cheeks
still rosy from the exertions of her Pilates
class. Her purse was over her shoulder
and she was reaching for the box of
granola bars on the counter when she

sensed a movement behind her. The dog?

No, it wasn't.

As Tanya turned, Coyle burst into the room and slashed her across the throat with a huge combat knife, blood spraying out of her like a broken sprinkler head. She dropped to the floor, clutching her throat. Her purse slid off her shoulder and spilled open as she fell.

Coyle reached down, grabbed her by an arm, and dragged her out of the kitchen, leaving a smeared swath of blood behind on the yellowed linoleum.

Eve stood there for a moment, surveying the blood spatter, freshly dripping down the cabinets in her imagination, and wondered again why Coyle slashed Tanya's throat rather than sexually assaulting her, the way he had with Vickie Denhoff.

She followed the trail of blood down the hall and peeked into the bathroom as she passed, seeing the dog's corpse in the bathtub, the white-tiled shower walls only spotted with blood. The real butchery hadn't begun yet.

When Eve got to the master bedroom, Coyle was straddling Tanya on the bed, stabbing her in a wild rage, ripping her and the mattress to shreds and splattering himself, the headboard, the walls and floor with her blood. Each stab into her body, each arc of his arm, lifting the knife up and down, sent drops of blood flying.

Eve turned and went back down the hall, fast-forwarding by hours, and getting to the front door just as Caitlin and Troy came in from school. They were shrugging off their backpacks when Coyle, drenched in blood and now wearing dish gloves, charged at them with the bloody knife he'd been using to dismember Tanya in the bathtub.

The children both screamed. Coyle pounced on Troy, stabbing him deep in the chest, killing the child instantly. Caitlin ran past him. Coyle yanked the knife from the boy and chased Caitlin down the hall. Eve followed them both.

Caitlin scampered into her room, jumped onto the bed, and struggled desperately to lift the double-sashed window. But it wouldn't move. Coyle burst in, grabbed her by the upper arm, lifted her off the bed like a rag doll, and slit her throat, the blood spraying the walls and her shelf of stuffed animals. He dropped her on the floor and lumbered out of her room to continue butchering her mother in the bathtub.

The image of Caitlin evaporated and Eve was left staring at the bloodstain on the floor where the child had bled out. Something about the chain of events didn't fit. It was something she felt rather than knew. *What was wrong with the scenario?*

Eve glanced at the bed. All the bedding was still there, except for the pillowcase, which she assumed CSU took with them for evidence analysis. Her gaze strayed to the headboard and the walls beside it. She didn't see any blood spatter, which struck her as odd. She bent down and examined the sheets and comforter. There was no blood there, either. *How did blood get on the pillowcase but not on anything else around it?*

She turned, faced the door, and began searching for any other blood drops she might have missed before. Her head was down, her attention focused on the walls and floor, and she bumped her side into the standing fan. She caught the fan before it fell and, while she was at it, examined the blades and grille to see if there was any blood on them and noticed the power cord dangling from the back of the unit. The cord appeared to be way too short. She gathered up the cord and came up with a ragged end. The plug was gone. The cord had been cut.

Eve was puzzling over that when she heard the front door open and a man's voice say: "Oh my God."

She hurried out of Caitlin's room into the hall and saw Jared Rawlins standing in the living room, staring wide-eyed and horrified at all the blood.

His gaze settled on her. "What did he do to them?"

Eve gently grasped his upper arm and tugged him toward the door. "Let's go outside, Mr. Rawlins. You don't need to see this."

He wrenched his arm free of her light grasp. "I lived with Tanya and her kids. They were part of my life . . . and you thought I could . . ." He struggled to find the right words, his eyes panning over the trails of blood on the floor, the streaks and splatter on the walls, before returning to her. ". . . *slaughter* them? Me?"

"I'm sorry," Eve said.

"It's worse than that. You actually believed I'd hack them up, splash my home in their blood and guts, and go back to a hotel in Lancaster for a good-morning fuck with a set decorator. What the hell is wrong with you?" Eve didn't answer him. There was nothing she could say. His eyes filled with tears and his face was pale. "It's a slaughterhouse and I haven't even left the living room yet. What am I going to see back there?"

He gestured down the hall.

"You don't want to see it, believe me," she said. "I can recommend a good crime scene cleaning service that will—"

Jared cut her off. "How am I supposed to live here now? How can *anyone* live here now?"

"I don't know."

They stood there for a long moment in silence. When Jared spoke again, it was in a near whisper. "Why are you here?"

"I wanted one more look to see if I missed anything," she said, which reminded her of something. "What happened to the fan?"

He stared at her like she was speaking a foreign language. "What?"

"The standing fan in Caitlin's room. The power cord was cut. I was wondering how it happened."

Now his uncomprehending stare turned into disbelief. "You see all of this, all the blood, and that's what's bothering you? What happened to her fan? Jesus Christ. Get out. Just . . . *get out*."

She wasn't upset about what he said because he was right. Because now that she thought about the fan cord, she couldn't get it out of her mind. It didn't fit. In fact, that wasn't the only thing that was nagging at her about what she saw in Caitlin's room. She needed to focus on that and not worry about how Jared was feeling right now, though seeing him reminded her that Tanya had been looking for a new place to live.

Eve walked past him and out the front door. She continued down the front walk to her car, the wind whipping up leaves all around her, took out her phone, and texted Nan.

**What did you find on Caitlin's pillowcase?**

She got into the car and, while she waited for a reply, called Duncan's cell. He answered on the second ring.

"Hey, Eve. What's up?"

"Did Biddle or Garvey ever talk to the Realtor that Tanya was supposed to meet on the day she was killed?"

"Hang on," Duncan said. Eve could hear phones ringing in the background and the indiscernible chatter of voices. It was like being on hold with customer support in Mumbai. He came back on a moment later. "No, they didn't. We zeroed in on Coyle before they got the chance to speak to her. But they did get her name and where she works."

"Let me have them both," Eve said.

She made a note of the information, thanked him, and was about to start the car when her phone vibrated to signal the arrival of a text. It was from Nan.

**Her pillow didn't have a pillowcase.**

There were a lot of reasons Caitlin might not have had a pillowcase on her pillow, but it still struck Eve as odd.

Eve texted.

Did Coyle take the pillowcases from
Tanya's bed?

Nan replied.

Yes. He took all of the bedding, most
likely because it was covered with blood
and perhaps his own DNA in the form of
semen, saliva, or body hair.

That made sense. It also explained why he left
Caitlin's bedding behind. There was no blood on
it.

*But did he take Caitlin's pillowcase? And if so,
why? Did he need it to carry something? If so,
what?*

It was frustrating. The last thing Eve needed
was more questions. What she wanted now were
answers.

# CHAPTER
# THIRTY-SEVEN

Parkway Realty was in an old storefront shopping center that had been remodeled to match the architectural style of the Commons and its Rolex clock tower across the street. The real estate office was tucked in a corner of the shopping center between a clothing store that sold $500 jeans and a bakery that sold $12 cupcakes, prices Eve would never pay for either item.

Eve badged the petite blonde twentysomething receptionist at Parkway's front desk, asked to see Donna Stokes, and was greeted instead by Clarissa Kelton, who introduced herself as the managing Realtor.

Clarissa was long limbed and long necked, her equine physique underscored by a Ralph Lauren polo shirt and the skintight Ariat horse-riding breeches that she was wearing. Eve was sure that Clarissa had a crop to go with the ensemble.

"How may I help you, Detective?" Clarissa asked, looking down her long, narrow nose at Eve.

"I'd like to talk with Donna Stokes."

"Donna hasn't been in for a few days. The last time I saw her was Monday, but I'm in and out a lot myself, showing houses." Clarissa turned to the receptionist. "How about you, Tess?"

"I don't go anywhere," Tess said. "I haven't seen her since Tuesday."

"Is it unusual for Donna not to visit the office for days?" Eve asked.

"Not really. Realtors aren't required to spend time in here. I have some who work almost entirely out of their cars," Clarissa said. "Donna could be out of town or maybe she got lucky. There was one time she hooked up with a guy on Tinder, a tantric sex instructor, and she didn't come up for air for three days."

"It's not as fun as it sounds," Tess said. "After a few hours, it starts to feel like constipation."

Clarissa regarded Tess with a raised, sharply tweezed eyebrow. "Is that so?"

Eve asked, "Do either of you have Donna's cell phone number and home address?"

"Her numbers are on her business card and I have her home address." Clarissa took out her phone to look up the address. "In fact, I sold her the house. It's what got her interested in real estate after her divorce. She sold cosmetics before that."

Tess handed Donna's business card to Eve. Clarissa showed her screen to Eve, who made a note of the address on the back of the card. Donna lived in Greater Mulwood, one of the first Calabasas housing tracts, off Mulholland Highway, near the Gelson's shopping center.

"Thank you," Eve said.

"Is Donna in some kind of trouble?" Clarissa asked.

"No, I just want to ask her some questions about one of her clients, Tanya Kenworth. Donna was helping her find a home to rent. Would you have any of that information here? Or Donna's calendar perhaps?"

"Donna would have all that and we don't have the password to her computer," Clarissa said.

"That's okay." Eve handed Clarissa and Tess each one of her cards. "Please have Donna call me if she checks in."

# CHAPTER
# THIRTY-EIGHT

Donna's house was a 1960s-era tract home that had been restored to its original midcentury modern style and bold colors: bright green, with white trim and red doors. The front courtyard was surrounded by see-through cinder block walls with white decorative gravel beds at their base. The other tract homes on the street had either been drastically remodeled and stripped of their midcentury architectural details or had been torn down and replaced with Spanish-Mediterranean-style homes with red tile roofs.

Eve parked in the driveway, knocked on the front door, and rang the bell, but there was no answer. The drapes were drawn on the windows and she didn't sense any sign of life. She pushed open the mail slot on the door and peeked inside. There was no mail on the floor, so unless Donna had filed a mail hold with the post office, somebody had been home in the last few days.

"What are you doing, lady?" asked a man behind her.

Eve stood up and turned around. A balding man in his sixties, wearing an untucked safari shirt with about thirty-seven pockets, cargo shorts with twelve more pockets, and a pair of flip-flops, stood on the sidewalk with his hands on his hips.

"I'm Detective Eve Ronin." She took out her badge and flashed it as she approached him. "Los Angeles County Sheriff's Department."

"We're colleagues," he said.

"We are?"

"I'm Irv Rothstein, commander of the Greater Mulwood Neighborhood Watch Patrol. That's why I was checking up on you. I live across the street." He jerked his thumb over his shoulder at a tract home with four obvious, poorly constructed room additions that hung on the house like the pockets on his cargo shorts. A placard in the window, shaped like a stop sign, said **THIS HOUSE IS PROTECTED BY NEIGHBORHOOD WATCH**. "We watch for intruders of all kinds, including coyotes."

"It's good that you keep a close eye on your homes. I'm looking for Donna Stokes. Have you seen her around?"

"Not since Wednesday. Her dog started barking early Thursday morning so I went in to check on him," he said. "It's not like Donna to leave Captain America in the house all day. The Captain pooped all over the living room, I'm talking big piles, and there wasn't any water in his bowl."

Eve's heart rate quickened. Donna had been gone since Wednesday, the day she was supposed

263

to meet Tanya to show her some rental homes, the same day the family was murdered. That couldn't possibly be a coincidence. The question was: What did it all mean?

"You have a key to her house?" Eve asked.

"Oh sure, and she has mine, too. We take care of each other's dogs when we go on vacations or if something comes up that keeps us away from home for too long. We can't keep our dogs outside because of the coyotes, so they're house dogs. The problem is, we can't be away for more than four or five hours or we're going to have a mess to clean up. We have shag carpet and the stains never go away."

"Donna didn't call you to say she'd be away?"

"No, she didn't and it makes no sense. She even calls if she has an unexpected amorous encounter, if you follow my meaning. Captain America has been over with Martha and me since Thursday. He's such a sweet dog. Snickerdoodle loves him. She's a French poodle."

"Did everything look okay inside Donna's house?" Eve asked.

"Besides the poop and the pee I had to clean up? Yeah, it was fine, but I'm not a fan of retro furniture. It was dated then and is even more dated now. Classic furniture never gets old. Always buy classic designs. I should know. I'm in the furniture business."

"Is her car in the garage?"

"Never," Irv said. "She uses the garage as a storage unit. It's wall-to-wall, floor-to-ceiling boxes of God knows what. She always parks in the driveway. That's the problem with these midcentury houses. All windows and no place to put anything."

Her car was gone, too. An idea was beginning to form in the back of Eve's mind about how this new information could factor into what happened to Tanya. "What kind of car does she drive?"

"A 2017 Mercedes E-class, metallic blue with a fancy license plate rim covered in fake Schwartzvasky crystals."

"Swarovski," Eve said.

"Whatever. I think it's garish. Captain America's collar has them, too, which is humiliating for a Doberman, especially one with that name," Irv said. "Is Donna in trouble?"

It was the same question Clarissa had asked. It's the same question most people asked whenever she started prodding them about someone. Eve didn't have a straight answer. Yes, she was sure Donna was in trouble, but what kind?

"No, I just want to ask her some questions about a friend of hers," Eve said and handed Irv her card. "Please ask Donna to give me a call when she gets home."

He stuck the card in one of his many shirt pockets. "I'll keep my eye out for her."

                                    • • •

Eve left the Mulwood neighborhood, turned north onto Mulholland Highway, and drove toward the **WELCOME TO CALABASAS** median boulder, where three days ago two LAPD detectives had tried to stick her and Duncan with a dead man in a pickup truck. His throat had been cut wide open.

The body was found on the same morning that the homicides of Tanya and her children were discovered. In fact, Eve realized, the truck was parked only a few yards from the Gelson's shopping center where the deputies gathered before serving the no-knock warrant at Coyle's house. They met there because it was the nearest rallying point for them near Coyle's house.

*Another odd coincidence. Or was it?*

Eve slammed on her brakes, coming to a jarring stop at the same spot where the LAPD cars had been parked the morning that she and Duncan had rolled up behind the dead man's truck.

Her heart was racing. She knew that she was onto something . . . but she wasn't sure what it was.

She looked across the flower-bed median at the northwest corner of Mulholland and Mulholland. There was an office building that was set back from the corner by a parking lot and a grove of pine trees. It was the spot where the pickup, its windshield splattered with blood, had been parked before the LAPD officer pushed it over the city limits into the Calabasas side of the road.

It struck Eve at the time, and again now, that the man had picked a strange place to slit his throat.

*Did his choice have something to do with the office building? Or was it the view of Gelson's? If he was murdered, by whom and why here of all places?*

She got out of her car and looked at what was on her side of the street. A cyclone fence surrounded a dense wooded patch of oaks and brittle, parched brush that covered the hillside. There was a dry creek down below that she assumed weaved its way along the base of the hills to Topanga Canyon.

Eve jumped up on the cyclone fence, easily scaled it, and dropped down on the hard dirt on the other side. She followed the arid creek bed east, past the fenced boundary of Louisville High School, a Roman Catholic girls' school, and then followed a deer path that cut through the weeds and brush, going up and across the steep hillside at an angle that made the ascent gradual and easy. She stopped and looked up to see what was at the top of the hill.

It was Coyle's mobile home park.

And high behind that, looming ominously above the Santa Monica Mountains to the southeast, was a massive, billowing cloud of roiling dark smoke.

Eve knew exactly what was burning and that it was her fault.

# CHAPTER
# THIRTY-NINE

Eve sat down on the hillside, closed her eyes, and tried to clear her head. It was as if every synapse in her brain was firing at once, a thousand firecrackers exploding, making her ears ring.

The discovery that the Realtor and her car were missing, and the proximity of the dead man in the truck to Coyle's mobile home, gave Eve a new, terrifying perspective on the murders. It was forcing her to rethink her assumptions, the meaning of the evidence they'd collected, and the significance of what she'd seen in her last walk-through of the house before Jared set it ablaze.

She was still trying to make sense of it all when her phone rang.

It was Duncan. "There's a huge fire in Topanga."

"I can see it," Eve said.

"You'll never guess where it started."

It pained her, but she knew. "Tanya's house."

She thought about what Jared told her: *How am I supposed to live here now? How can anyone live here now?*

"After you left, Jared soaked it in gasoline and set it on fire. He's in custody, but by the time the fire department got up there, the wind had whipped the blaze into a firestorm. The blaze is moving like a tidal wave. They've closed Topanga State Park. Our search parties have been called in and all of our deputies have been reassigned to assist the fire department with evacuating homes and controlling traffic."

"Jared was distraught when I saw him," Eve said. "I should never have left him alone in the house. I should have seen this coming."

"How? Are you psychic? Omniscient? People do crazy things when they are emotionally distressed. You can't be expected to predict it all and you aren't responsible for any of it. If you start blaming yourself for every stupid thing that people do during an investigation, you'll either quit the job or become an alcoholic."

"So you just shrug and move on?"

"Sometimes I'll shake my head instead. Or if I'm really unhinged, I might do both. Where are you?"

"Mulholland and Mulholland. I'm chasing a new lead."

"The Realtor gave you something?"

"You could say that," she said. "Where can I find those two lazy assholes we met here from the LAPD?"

The Topanga Community Police Station was off Canoga Avenue, around the corner from the Xposed Gentleman's Club, and boasted drought-resistant landscaping, green energy design, and a vaulted glass atrium lobby. If it wasn't for all the police vehicles in the lot, Eve could have mistaken the $36 million complex for a neighborhood library.

The officer at the front desk was black and his uniform was crisply pressed, the creases so sharp that Eve thought they could be used to slice meat. She flashed her badge as she approached.

"Hello, I'm Detective Eve Ronin, Los Angeles County Sheriff's Department. I need to see Frank Knobb or Arnie Prescott."

The officer examined her ID for a moment, then picked up his phone, dialed a three-digit extension, and said: "This is Officer Lofland at the front desk. The Deathfist is here to see you." He met her eye as he listened to the reply. "Yes, she's actually standing right here . . . will do."

He hung up the phone and handed Eve a clip-on visitor's pass. "Detective Knobb says to go on back. It's through that door, then it's the third door on your left."

"Thanks," she said and clipped the badge to her belt. The officer buzzed her through a door on the far side of the lobby.

Knobb was waiting for her in the hallway, outside the door to the detective bureau. "Now this is a surprise. Shouldn't you be in Beverly Hills today, meeting with your agents at CAA?"

"I'm working a triple homicide."

"Yeah, I know, I saw the press conference. It was the first night in weeks there wasn't anything on the news about the indictment of those deputies at the Men's Central Jail."

Eve ignored the dig and pressed on. As much as she disliked and disrespected this man, she needed his help. "I think the dead guy you found in the truck on Thursday may be connected to our case."

"How?"

"I don't know yet."

Knobb smirked, crossed his arms under his chest, and leaned his shoulder against the wall. "You know what I think? You're feeding me a line of bullshit. You're eager for another murder to solve to capitalize on your moment in the spotlight and this corpse happens to be handy."

"So you haven't closed it yet."

He straightened up, taking a more defensive posture. "Don't sound so hopeful. You aren't getting the case. You'll have to wait for a body to drop in your jurisdiction."

She resisted the urge to remind him that he was being very protective of a case that he'd pushed into her jurisdiction just a few days ago but she didn't think that would be a persuasive argument. So she took a different approach.

"The morning after three people were murdered and dismembered with a knife, your victim was found with his throat slit in a truck parked a hundred yards from where our killer lives. I think that's a mighty big coincidence, don't you?" Eve said. Knobb pursed his lips, considering the implications. "I don't want your case, Frank. I just need to know what you've got. What's the harm in telling me? We both want the same thing here, to catch whoever killed him."

Knobb sighed in resignation and gestured for her to follow him into the detective bureau. The cubicles were large, each with Plexiglas dividers on two sides that created a more open feel around sleek curved desks with flat-screen monitors and stylish ergonomic desk chairs. He sat down at his cubicle, wheeled over a chair for her, and she sat down.

"The victim's name is Roger Karpis," Knobb said. "He works at Malibu Creek State Park."

She was familiar with Malibu Creek State Park. It was eight thousand acres of peaks, canyons, rolling hills, and meadows south of Mulholland Highway and west of Las Virgenes. It was originally owned by 20th Century Fox, which used it as various locations for hundreds of movies and television shows. The studio donated the property in the mid-'70s to the state, which opened it to the public as a park, but there were film crews in there shooting on almost a daily basis. Some deputies, like Garvey, made extra cash off-hours working as set security. The Paramount Ranch bordered the northwest end of the park and also doubled as a shooting location and state recreation area.

"Karpis was a forest ranger?" Eve asked.

"More like a night watchman. The park is popular with campers and film crews. His job was to make sure nobody burns the place down or vandalizes any movie sets during the night." Knobb clicked a few keys and brought up on his screen some gruesome pictures of the victim and his gaping neck wound. "We quickly ruled out suicide. Somebody in the passenger seat pulled Roger's head back and slit his throat, practically to the spine. We're thinking it was a hitchhiker, maybe a prostitute."

"I've never heard of hookers hanging out on Mulholland."

"That's not how it's done in upscale neighborhoods. They use apps or social media to book anonymous sex," Knobb said. "We know from Roger's friends and family that he was dealing with a sex addiction problem. Getting blow jobs and hand jobs in parking lots was one of his favorite pastimes."

"Was his wallet or phone taken?"

Knobb shook his head. "We're thinking the killer must have been spooked by someone or something. We don't have much to go on."

"Can you show me the interior of the truck?" Eve asked. Knobb scrolled through pictures of the bloody cab and the large knife on the passenger seat. She tapped the screen. "Has the knife been confirmed as the murder weapon?"

"Yes, it has."

"It was nice of the killer to leave it behind."

"We're thinking that maybe it belonged to Roger and he had it in the truck, maybe under the passenger seat or something, and the killer grabbed it as a weapon of opportunity," Knobb said. "It's an SOG Jungle Primitive knife, a popular choice among ISIS members for beheading captives."

"Did you get any prints from it?"

"Nope," he said.

"I'd like that knife sent to our crime scene unit for analysis," she said. The knife wouldn't have to go far, perhaps just across a room. The LAPD and LASD shared crime lab facilities within the California Forensic Institute on the campus of California State University in Monterey Park.

"You think you're going to find the DNA of your three victims in the hilt of the knife?" Knobb asked.

Yes, she did, and DNA from Donna Stokes, too.

"I think it's worth checking," Eve said. "If I'm right, you can say the LAPD provided the key clue that closed a triple murder that baffled the sheriff's department."

Eve was still missing key evidence, but she now believed that the Realtor showed up at Tanya's house on Wednesday morning . . . and walked in on a nightmare. Coyle killed Stokes and used *her* car to dispose of the bodies. That was why his car was clean.

Knobb regarded her with an appraising gaze. "You weren't baffled. You knew what you were going to find before you walked in here. All I did was confirm it and give you a few more facts."

"That's true," she said. "But that spin won't help you much, will it?"

"We're going to look good at your expense."

"I don't care."

"The sheriff might," he said.

"All that matters to me is what's good for the case," she said. "Besides, now you'll owe me two favors."

"How do you figure *two?*"

She gave him a stern look. "Have you forgotten how we met?"

"I'll have the knife sent over to your CSU," he said.

"Can you email me the photos you showed me of Roger and the knife?"

"Sure," he said. "I'll do it now."

Eve thanked him and hurried out of the station as fast as she could without actually running. Because with each passing second, the realization of what really happened on that bloody, horrible Wednesday in Topanga was coming to her in revelations that felt like body blows. So much of what they thought they knew about what happened in Tanya's house was wrong.

The moment Eve stepped outside, she looked to the south. The smoke from the Topanga fire loomed over the Santa Monica Mountains like huge, vicious storm clouds seething with thunderous fury. It terrified her.

She took out her phone, googled the Wikipedia listing for the original *Planet of the Apes* movie, and scrolled through the post to the section labeled "Production Information." One line jumped out at her:

> Most of the scenes of the ape village, interiors and exteriors, were filmed on the Fox Ranch in Malibu Creek State Park, northwest of Los Angeles.

It was the same park where Roger worked.

*That* was the key piece that she'd been missing.

Now she knew how the ranger's truck ended up at the corner of Mulholland and Mulholland and why Coyle had killed him.

But it was everything else that was becoming clear to her now, all of the wrong assumptions that she'd made, that was threatening to cripple her with panic and fear.

*How could I have been so blind and stupid?*

Eve called Duncan and cut him off before he could finish saying hello. "I need to see you, the captain, and the sheriff immediately. It's an emergency. If either of them argue with you, tell them their careers will be ruined and more people will die if they don't get their asses to the station right now."

"What have you found?" Duncan asked.

"We got it all wrong," she said. "And we're running out of time."

She hung up, got into her car, and raced back to Lost Hills with her siren on, lights flashing, and gas pedal pressed to the floor, running red lights and weaving through traffic. It took her seventeen minutes to travel thirteen miles.

Eve arrived at the station, coming to a tire-squealing stop, just as an LASD chopper was landing on the helipad. It was the sheriff. She ran into the station, pretending not to hear him shout her name over the whirring of the chopper blades.

She went straight to the squad room, rushed past Duncan, and ripped the crime scene photos that she needed from the dry-erase board, gathered them under her arm, then turned to face her confused partner.

"Where are we meeting?" she demanded, breathing hard.

"In the captain's office," Duncan said.

"Let's go."

She hurried down the hall, throwing open the captain's door without knocking, to find Moffett and Lansing standing there. Both men were furious. Lansing immediately confronted her.

"What's so Goddamn important that I had to drop everything to get here?" He pointed out the captain's window. "There's a firestorm raging behind us. Three thousand acres have gone up in flames in the lasts few hours and we're evacuating hundreds of homes. If the fire meets up with the Stevenson blaze, which is rampaging into Simi Valley now towards the Pacific, we could have one of the worst fires in state history. What do you have to tell us that's a bigger emergency than *that?*"

"We screwed up the triple murder investigation, sir," she said. "We got it wrong."

"Are you saying Lionel Coyle didn't butcher those people?"

"That's the one thing we got right," she said.

"Then why the hell are we here?"

"Because there's still a chance that we can save Caitlin Kenworth's life."

# CHAPTER FORTY

The three men stared at her like she'd gone insane. She was expecting that reaction. It was Moffett who spoke first, in a slow, patronizing tone that was filled with disdain.

"I don't see how we can save her," he said. "She's already been killed and hacked into pieces."

"She's alive," Eve insisted. "At least she was on Wednesday and I'm hoping she still is today. Coyle took her. This triple murder was actually a child abduction. It was all along. That's what we missed."

Duncan sat down. "I'm confused."

"Join the damn club," Lansing said, taking a seat as well. "Make it fast, Ronin. Every minute we sit here another five acres goes up in flames."

"I'm well aware of that," Eve said. "It's why we have to act fast."

"The blood evidence is conclusive," Moffett said. "Three people were killed."

"That's true," Eve said. "I'm not disputing that."

Moffett took a seat behind his desk, leaving only Eve standing.

"If Caitlin is still alive," Duncan said, "then who is the third person who got killed in Tanya's house?"

"Donna Stokes, the Realtor who was going to help Tanya find a new home to rent," Eve said. "Donna has been missing since Wednesday. I think she walked in on Tanya being killed and it's *her* blood in Caitlin's room. That also explains why we found no blood or anything else in Coyle's car. He used Donna's car to take away Caitlin, the body parts, and other evidence from the house."

The sheriff massaged his brow. "You're not making any sense."

"The evidence was all there from the start but we misread it." Eve set her stack of photos on Moffett's desk and hastily sorted through them until she found the one she wanted. She held up a crime scene photo of Caitlin's room. "Take a look at this. The pillowcase is missing from Caitlin's bed. The assumption was that Coyle took it. But why would he do that?"

"He was cleaning up evidence," Duncan said.

"Of what?" Eve said. "The blood is on the floor and the walls. There is no blood spatter on the bed or the headboard . . . so there wasn't any on the pillowcase. It's gone because he used it to cover Caitlin's head."

"That's a big leap," Moffett said.

She pointed to the standing fan, tapping it with her finger. "We missed this fan. The power cord is cut off. That's because he used the cord to bind her."

Eve tossed the photo across the desk to Moffett

and pulled another one from her stack, holding it up in front of each man in turn. It was a picture of the bloody print left on the floor by one of Caitlin's shoes.

"This print from Caitlin's shoe was found in the hallway near the garage. The bloody print is tainted with cleaner and motor oil, so we know it was made *after* the killings. We assumed her shoe fell out of one of the trash bags Coyle lugged out," she said. "We were wrong. Caitlin put her foot down for a moment as she was being carried away. That's proof of life."

"Or it's proof that a shoe fell out of a trash bag," Lansing said.

Eve tossed the photo back on the desk, found another picture, and thrust it in Lansing's face. "We also have this."

It was a picture of a spec of blood on the wall. Lansing squinted at it. "Looks like just another spot of blood to me."

"This one is different," she said. "It's undiluted and on the wall near the footprint. It's Caitlin's blood."

"How do you know that?" Moffett said.

"Because Duncan saw Coyle naked and he didn't have a cut on him," Eve said.

"Not that I could see," Duncan said.

"It would need to be a big cut, on his head or arm, to leave a fresh spot of blood on the wall as he passed by. Did you see a cut like that?"

"No," Duncan said.

"That's why I know it's Caitlin's blood. She must have been cut by Coyle during a struggle, or he cut her to prove he was serious, like he did with the woman he raped," Eve said. "The DNA results on that spot of blood, and the blood found in Caitlin's room, will prove I'm right, but by then it will be too late to save her."

"It already is," Moffett said. "Caitlin is dead. She has been since Wednesday."

Eve ignored him and turned to Duncan. "Remember what you said when you saw the surveillance video at Walmart and all the junk food that Coyle bought?"

"He eats like a kid," Duncan said.

"That's because he wasn't buying the food for himself, he was buying it for her," Eve said. "The *Planet of the Apes* DVD he bought there was for her, too."

"Eve, I know you want her to be alive," Duncan said. "We all wish she was. But she's not."

She looked at the faces of the three men and saw nothing but skepticism and sadness. They didn't believe her. She knew the sheriff and the captain would be a hard sell, but she was counting on Duncan to be on her side. And he wasn't.

Duncan sighed. "You need to take a deep breath and be reasonable about this. You're seeing what you want to see . . . but it isn't there."

She wasn't going to give up. She couldn't. Not while there was a chance of saving Caitlin.

Eve took out her phone and swiped through the pictures that Knobb sent her until she found one of Roger Karpis' gaping neck wound. She held up her phone and showed the picture to the men as she spoke.

"This man is Roger Karpis, a ranger at Malibu Creek State Park, where *Planet of the Apes* was shot. His body was left in a pickup truck sometime Wednesday night or Thursday morning on Mulholland at Mulholland, which is only a hundred yards from where Coyle lives."

She swiped to a photo of the bloody knife on the passenger seat and showed it around. Lansing studied it.

"This is the knife that nearly took off the ranger's head. It's the knife that Coyle used to murder Tanya, Troy, and Donna," she said. "I've had it sent to our lab. The DNA tests will prove me right . . . but it will be too late."

"I'm not seeing what this all means," Lansing said and handed the photo back to her.

"Because it doesn't mean a thing," Moffett said.

She took a deep breath and let it out slowly.

"Here is what happened. Donna Stokes walked in on Coyle butchering Tanya. Coyle killed Stokes in Caitlin's room and cut her up, too. He was still at it when Caitlin and Troy came home from school. Coyle killed the boy but kept Caitlin alive. He tied Caitlin up with the fan cord and put the pillowcase over her head. Coyle used Donna Stokes' Mercedes to stash Caitlin somewhere and to dispose of the bodies at the ruins of the old *Planet of the Apes* set in Malibu Creek State Park. That's when the ranger stumbled on Coyle, who forced him at knifepoint to drive him nearly home."

Duncan nodded, thinking it through. "So you think Coyle killed the ranger to keep him quiet, left the knife behind in the truck, and walked back to his place. From there, he either walked or rode a bike to the Topanga trailhead where his Toyota was parked. That's why the Toyota was clean."

"Yes," Eve said, encouraged that Duncan was at least following the evidence. "The ranger was in the wrong place at the wrong time. Coyle had to kill him to cover up his crimes. But the ranger showing up was also a golden opportunity for Coyle. The ranger gave Coyle a way to get home without using Donna's car, which could forensically link him to the murders at Tanya's house if he was caught driving the Mercedes or if it was found near his place. The car is probably still somewhere in or near Malibu Creek State Park and close to wherever Caitlin is trapped."

"My God, Ronin," Moffett said, shaking his

head. "Listen to yourself. Your story is getting crazier by the minute."

"It's not crazy. It all fits. Coyle has been arrested twice for masturbating in public while watching young girls, and those are just the two instances that we know about. He lives right behind a school for girls, so I suspect there are a lot more cases where he wasn't caught," Eve said. "On top of that, he's obsessed with a movie where humans are kept as house pets."

"Telling me he's a pervert with an ape obsession doesn't mean he's capable of plotting the elaborate scheme you've just laid out," Moffett said. "In fact, it argues persuasively against it."

Eve slapped the stack of photos on Moffett's desk. "I'm telling you Caitlin is stashed somewhere, probably in a house near Malibu Creek State Park that Coyle visited before on a service call."

"Eve," Duncan began, but she cut him off, whirling around to face him.

"Don't you see, Duncan? That's what I got wrong when I interrogated Coyle. I said we were looking for Tanya, Caitlin, and Troy's body parts. He knew we didn't know that she was still alive. That's why he perked up. That's also why Coyle wanted to meet with us this morning. He's worried about Caitlin, too. He's convinced he's going to walk and wants it to happen today, while there's a chance that she's still alive."

"You've convinced me," Lansing said.

Eve turned, stunned. She was certain Duncan would be the first one she convinced and he'd help her win over the others. Perhaps she'd underestimated the sheriff. But she wasn't the only one who was surprised. So was the captain.

Moffett looked at Lansing in disbelief. "You can't be serious, sir."

"I think she's right. Coyle killed the ranger and the body parts we're looking for are buried somewhere in Malibu Creek State Park." Lansing turned to Eve. "That was brilliant detective work, Ronin. You never cease to amaze me."

"We need to send deputies to every house Mr. Plunger sent Coyle to near Malibu Creek State Park," Eve said.

"Whoa, hold up, Ronin," Lansing said, raising his hands in a halting gesture. "I'm with you on the bodies. But your theory about Caitlin is wishful thinking, to put it kindly. I'll chalk it up to exhaustion and heartbreak. It's a horrific case and I don't blame you for dreaming of a happy ending."

Eve felt her face flushing with anger, enraged by his lack of understanding and his patronizing lecture. How could he believe only part of what she'd told him? Recovering Caitlin was far more important than the bodies.

"But Donna Stokes is missing, and all the forensic evidence proves that Caitlin—"

"Nothing different than what we first assumed," Lansing interrupted. "But even if I thought that Caitlin might be alive, and I don't, it's too dangerous to go up there right now for any reason."

"We have to take that chance," Eve said.

"It's an inferno," Lansing said. "We'll send search parties into Malibu Creek Park, and deputies out to the adjacent homes that Coyle visited, to look for the bodies as soon as the fire department says it's safe."

Eve shook her head in defiance. "No, sir, that's unacceptable. We have to act now. Caitlin is out there, trapped and alone. We can't leave her to die from dehydration or fire."

"You aren't hearing me." Lansing stood up and got right into her face. "She is already dead. You are not to suggest otherwise to anyone or I will take your badge. Do you understand me? It would be unspeakably cruel to give the family false hope."

"It would be worse to let her die," Eve said and stormed out of the captain's office, slamming the door behind her.

# CHAPTER FORTY-ONE

Eve ran out of the station, jumped into the plain-wrap Explorer, and sped to her condo, double-parked at the curb, and dashed inside to grab her list of Coyle's service calls and get another look at the pushpins in her map. She couldn't sit back and let Caitlin die, not if there was still a chance of saving her.

Malibu Creek State Park was bordered by Mulholland Highway to the north; Crags Road, Lake Vista Drive, and its offshoots to the west; and Las Virgenes Road to the east. The only homes that directly bordered the park were on Lake Vista, Crags Road, and the neighborhoods that rimmed the eastern edge of Malibu Lake.

She checked the map, and then the list, quickly identified six homes that Coyle visited adjacent to the park, and wrote the addresses on a slip of paper that she stuffed in her pocket. Now she just had to get to the houses, which wasn't going to be easy, and then deal with smoke and possibly fire when she got there to search for Caitlin.

She opened the closet under her stairs, grabbed the fire extinguisher and her earthquake kit, which was a duffel bag full of supplies that included goggles, leather gloves, dust masks, a first aid kit, and a crowbar, and rushed out of the house.

As soon as she got into the Explorer, she tossed her bag and the extinguisher on the passenger seat and tuned in to the LASD patrol frequency to hear the latest news about the fire, evacuations, and road closures.

She learned that the sheriff wasn't exaggerating about the voracious ferocity of the blaze. The fire was devouring acres by the minute, driven by single-digit humidity and blistering fifty-mile-per-hour winds. The tsunami of flames had already crossed Topanga Canyon and raged west across ten miles of mostly uninhabited wilds, eating up the parched plants for fuel and building in intensity as it jumped across Las Virgenes into Malibu Creek State Park. Officials were terrified that the Stevenson Ranch blaze, now moving through Ahmanson Ranch, could connect with the Topanga blaze to create a megafire if they weren't stopped.

Eve made a sharp U-turn on Las Virgenes, hit the siren and grille flashers, and took the 101 four miles west to the Kanan Dume Road exit. Along the way, she stole glances to her left at the thick, churning cloud of smoke that filled the sky behind the Santa Monica Mountains.

She got off at Kanan, turned left, crossed through the northbound stream of ash-covered vehicles packed with people, pets, and possessions escaping from the fire, and sped south on the overpass.

Sawhorse barricades at Agoura Road prevented vehicles from heading south on Kanan and two deputies stood in the intersection, directing all the traffic onto the freeway. But the deputies saw her coming in fast and furious. One deputy held up traffic for her while another moved a sawhorse aside so she could pass.

She waved her thanks to the deputies and hugged the southbound shoulder because both lanes on Kanan were filled with cars fleeing the fire zone. Water-dumping helicopters streaked overhead to the front line of the fire, only a few miles southeast.

A quarter mile south of Agoura Road, she cut across Kanan to Cornell Road, forcing the cars full of desperate evacuees to let her slip through with insistent blurts of her siren.

Eve sped down the narrow rural residential street and plowed through the curtain of smoke. Day suddenly became night, the sun almost entirely blotted out by the clouds of ash and swirling embers.

Twenty yards ahead, at the far edge of her diminishing field of visibility, an LASD patrol car was parked across the road as a barricade. A deputy, his face covered with a bandana, got out of the car and held up his hand for her to stop.

Eve rolled down the window just enough so she could hear him talk. Smoke seeped into the Explorer.

"You have to turn around," the deputy said. "The whole area south of here is under mandatory evacuation."

"I know," she said. "I've been sent to check for stragglers and convince them to get the hell out, forcibly if necessary."

"They'd be insane to stay. The fire is vast and out of control here. Even the firefighters are retreating in a few minutes to make their stand down at Malibu Lake and further west on Mulholland."

"I'll be right behind you with anybody I've found," she said.

He stepped out of her way and she drove past, slower now, moving through the dense fog of ash and embers, toward Mulholland Highway. She was in a race against time but she didn't want to mow down any firefighters in her haste.

The road was awash in a flurry of blazing embers that was igniting the dry brush all around her. To her right, a meadow in Paramount Ranch looked like it was alight with dozens of campfires. To her left, on a slight rise, an entire house was ablaze, abandoned by firefighters who were now in full retreat, rolling up their water lines and piling into their trucks. The house was a lost cause and there was nothing they could do now to prevent the firestorm from advancing. They'd have to make their stand farther west.

The firefighters were leaving, but she was going in. She knew it was dangerous, but she didn't have a choice. Caitlin was out there and Eve wasn't leaving without her.

# CHAPTER
# FORTY-TWO

Eve crossed Mulholland Highway and glanced to the east, where everything was aflame against a dark sky of billowing ash. There was a terrifying beauty to the flaming landscape—the snow-flurry of embers, trees turned into towers of fire, the little bonfires everywhere. It was like Christmas in Hell.

The first house on her list was off of Lake Vista, though there was no lake to be seen today. It was a Spanish-Mediterranean McMansion with a four-car garage, a cobblestone motor court, and a row of pine trees ringing the property that were fully engulfed in flames, bombarding the house with embers.

She put on her LASD baseball cap, the pair of goggles, and a dust mask, grabbed the crowbar, and dashed up to the house. It was like running through a storm of hot needles. The front door was ajar. She pushed it open the rest of the way, rushed across the two-story foyer and into a large open-concept kitchen and family room. It was immediately clear to her that the house had been recently occupied by a large family. The marble-topped island in the kitchen was the center of the family's life and was covered with the day's mail, the morning newspapers, and cereal boxes. There were children's toys scattered on the family room floor. Coyle couldn't have been using this house to hold Caitlin captive. It was occupied. Whoever lived here had just left in a hurry.

It took Eve less than sixty seconds to make that determination and then run back outside. But in that short time, the fire had reached the house, igniting the wood under the eaves and the dried pine needles in the rain gutters.

She jumped back into her car, made a fast three-point turn, and sped out onto the road to hit the next house on her list—located on a private lane off of Lake Vista, only a quarter of a mile away.

The smoke was even thicker now, swirling around her car, making it difficult to see. She caught a movement out of the corner of her eye and slammed on her brakes, nearly hitting a deer on fire, the shrieking animal charging across the road directly in front of her. The blazing deer tripped in a culvert, tumbled into the brush, and instantly ignited it.

Eve couldn't allow herself to be distracted by the horrific sight and drove on as fast as she could given her limited visibility. It was so hard to see that she almost passed the road she was looking for and would have if not for the cluster of mailboxes on the corner. She made a sharp left onto the narrow, poorly maintained road, bouncing hard into every pothole and over every bump, through a tunnel of flames, embers, and smoke.

At the end of the tunnel, she could see a sprawling ranch-style home surrounded by tall, dry weeds. It might as well have been in a pond of gasoline. As Eve got closer, she could see there was a car parked in front of the house. It was a metallic-blue 2017 Mercedes E-class, the fire on the roadway making the fake Swarovski crystals sparkle around the license plate. The car belonged to Donna Stokes, the missing Realtor.

*Caitlin was here.*

Eve knew she didn't have much time. The flames were closing in and the house was a tinderbox. She pulled up beside the car, grabbed her crowbar, and got out, leaving the motor running. She ran up to the front door and tried the knob. It was locked. She wedged the crowbar between the door and the jamb, put her full body weight into the bar, and split open the door.

The house was empty and unfurnished, the hardwood floors covered with a fine layer of dust. Cobwebs filled the spaces between the wooden beams on the pitched ceilings. The smell of burning wood was everywhere.

"Caitlin!" Eve yelled as she dashed through the house, checking every cabinet or closet that a child might fit in and finding only dust and rat droppings. "Caitlin!"

She ended up in the family room, where she stopped cold.

The room was furnished with a couch, a coffee table, a rug, and an old TV set with a DVD player on top. There were cases of bottled water stacked against one wall.

A sleeping bag, the one Eve had seen on the hill overlooking Tanya's house, was on the couch. An empty bag of Doritos, Ding Dong wrappers, and discarded Coke cans were on the coffee table . . . and so was an open *Planet of the Apes* DVD case, the disc missing. There was no doubt now that Coyle had brought Caitlin here.

*But where was she?*

"Caitlin!" Eve yelled out again. She went back through the house, checking each room again, but finding no sign of the child.

She peered outside one of the bedroom windows and saw a wave of fire coming toward the house, driven by wind and fueled by the dry brush on the abandoned property. Breaks in the smoke allowed her to see a large field between the back of the house and a rocky hillside a hundred yards away.

Eve went back to the family room and sat down on the couch. The flames licked the windows on one side of the house and the crackle of fire sounded like a monster gnashing its teeth.

She took a deep breath, closed her eyes, and let

her breath out slowly, forcing herself to be calm, to clear her head so she could think.

*Caitlin is here. Where is she hidden?*

Eve opened her eyes and scanned the room for any tells. There was no fresh paint or patching on the walls. The floors were covered with dust except for a path, made by herself and probably Coyle, from the front door to the rug.

*Why did he bring a rug?*

She bolted from the couch, grabbed the corner of the rug, and yanked it away, revealing a fresh sheet of plywood nailed to the floor. Eve jammed the crowbar under the plywood and forced it loose, the nails squealing like live animals as they were yanked from the joists, and lifted the sheet away.

Caitlin, in soiled clothes, her limbs bound tightly with duct tape, was wedged faceup between two joists. Another piece of duct tape, with a hole cut through for an IV tube, covered her mouth. The tube ran from her mouth to an empty bottle of water wedged between her head and the next joist. Her eyes were closed but she was breathing.

Eve's instinct was to immediately lift Caitlin from her cramped space. But the cop in her remembered that this was a crime scene, one that might soon be destroyed. She took out her phone, snapped a couple quick pictures of Caitlin, then gently peeled the tape from the child's mouth and removed the straw.

Eve leaned in close and carefully slipped her hands under Caitlin, who reeked of urine and sweat.

"I'm Eve. I'm a police officer. You're safe now."

Caitlin's eyelids fluttered open and she stared at Eve.

"Where is the monster?" she asked in a weak, raspy voice.

"Where he can't hurt you anymore."

Eve glanced out the window. The flames were everywhere. "I don't have time to untie you. I'm sorry. We have to go as fast as we can."

She picked the girl up, held her close, and ran for the front door into a wailing firestorm of embers, smoke, and ash. Tall, scorching flames were blowing against one side of the house and splashing like waves against the Mercedes, which formed a wall that protected the Explorer from the fire.

Eve opened the back door of the SUV, laid Caitlin down on the seat, belted her in, then got into the driver's seat and grabbed the radio.

"This is 22-David-4 requesting emergency rescue and fire department support. I'm at 74 Castlemere Road with a ten-year-old girl who is in need of immediate medical attention."

The dispatcher responded almost immediately. "Copy 22-David-4. Stand by."

Eve assessed her grim situation. The brush

around the house was ablaze. She glanced in the rearview mirror. The road behind her was a wall of flame, burning trees falling across the roadway, kicking up blasts of embers. It was impassable. She remembered the field behind the house and, behind it, the rocky hillside, but it was all hidden by a curtain of smoke. Was it already on fire?

"22-David-4," the dispatcher said. "Ground rescue isn't possible. Air support is en route. Can you get to an open field or to higher ground?"

"I'll find a way," Eve said.

She secured her seat belt, turned on the headlights, backed up, then put the car into drive, pressed the gas pedal to the floor, and charged into the curtain of smoke, bursting through the brown haze into the tall, thick, brittle brush. The field wasn't on fire yet, but it soon would be. The tall vegetation and smoke made it virtually impossible to see what she was driving into but she had no choice but to venture on as fast as she could. The Explorer bounced violently on hardscrabble dirt, through the bushes and weeds, jostling her hard from side to side.

"I apologize about the rough ride," Eve said to Caitlin. "It will be over soon."

She wrestled to control the car and peered intently into the dense smoke, hoping for a break that would show her the way. Instead, a tree broke through the haze like a runaway freight train. She yanked the wheel hard to the right, sideswiping the tree and shearing off her mirror.

Within seconds of avoiding the tree, the Explorer slammed into a boulder hidden by the brush and came to a brutal stop. The airbag exploded in Eve's face, stunning her.

It took a long second for Eve to regain her senses. Blood ran down her forehead. The front end of the Explorer was crumpled. The car wasn't going anywhere. She looked over her shoulder into the back seat.

Somehow Caitlin had ended up on the floor. She was crying, but otherwise unhurt.

"We're going to be okay," Eve said, and looked out the back window. The house was consumed by fire, igniting the brush behind them, the voracious flames moving at incredible speed in their direction. She reached out for the radio and felt a pain so sharp, intense, and unexpected that she choked back a scream.

Her right wrist was broken and she knew how it had happened. She'd been gripping the steering wheel hard when the collision happened and the airbag blasted open against her rigid arm. It was a common injury, but that knowledge didn't make it any less painful or inconvenient now. There was no time to make a brace. She'd have to power through it.

She picked up the radio with her left hand. "22-

David-4. We're going on foot, heading south of the house."

There was no response. Eve could only hope that someone heard what she'd said. She got out of the car, opened the back door, and reached down to pick up Caitlin, bracing herself for the agony.

It felt like an iron spike was driven into her arm. She gritted her teeth against the pain, lifted up the child, and tried to shift most of Caitlin's dead weight onto her left arm.

"I've got you," Eve said. "I'm not going to let you go."

She didn't know if she was trying to reassure Caitlin or herself but they could both use it.

Eve trudged forward through the brush, moving as fast as she could without tripping, hearing the crackling and feeling the heat on her back of the firestorm closing in. Blood from her scalp rolled into her eyes, stinging and blinding her, but she kept on. Her right wrist felt like it might snap off and that the only thing holding it together against the child's weight and the sheer agony was Eve's unbending will.

*There's no fucking way I'm dropping this child.*

*There's no fucking way I'm letting that fire catch us.*

She stumbled on a gopher hole, staggered to maintain her balance, and couldn't help crying out with pain when Caitlin's full weight momentarily shifted to her broken wrist. Eve wasn't sure whether it was tears or streams of blood that were running down her cheeks. It may have been both.

But then she heard the *whap-whap-whap* of a helicopter approaching. She stopped to look over her shoulder. A water-dropping helicopter came up behind them and doused the leading edge of the flames, buying Eve and Caitlin some time.

The helicopter banked away and a moment later a larger Los Angeles County Fire Department rescue chopper appeared overhead, its rotors whipping up the air all around them as it descended into the field a few yards ahead of her.

Two firefighters immediately leaped out of the open side door and rushed up to Eve. One firefighter took Caitlin from her and the other clutched Eve by her left forearm and led her quickly to the chopper. They climbed on board, where two emergency medical technicians waiting inside laid Caitlin on a gurney.

A firefighter buckled Eve into her seat. She braced her limp right arm with her left hand, hoping to ease the pain caused by each movement of her body or the aircraft.

The chopper rose up and banked over the abandoned house, which was fully engulfed in flames, then high over Malibu Creek State Park, much of it a sea of fire, then headed north toward

West Hills Hospital, the nearest emergency medical facility.

Eve looked over at the EMTs, one of whom leaned over Caitlin, cutting away the duct tape that bound her while the other prepared an IV.

A firefighter gently wiped the blood and dirt from around her eyes with moist pieces of cotton and yelled, so Eve would hear him over the rotors: "You're crazy, you know that?"

She glanced down at Caitlin and decided that maybe being crazy was necessary now and then.

# CHAPTER
# FORTY-THREE

"You're insane," Lisa said, applying the final layer of moist blue fiberglass tape to Eve's short-arm cast. It was perhaps the fifth or sixth time her sister had shared that observation, in one form or another, since Eve came into the West Hills Hospital ER. Eve had lost count of how many other people had expressed the same sentiment over the last two hours.

Eve sat on the edge of the gurney and looked across the chaotic ER full of firefighters and civilians injured in the blaze to the set of closed doors where doctors, an LASD detective experienced in crimes against children, and a Los Angeles County caseworker from Child Protective Services were taking care of Caitlin.

The child hadn't said a word since they'd fled the house and Eve hadn't asked her any questions. But Eve had stayed by Caitlin's side, refusing treatment for herself, until she was certain that the child was in good hands.

Caitlin was safe now, but Eve couldn't get the image of the little girl wedged between those floor joists out of her mind. She'd rescued Caitlin, but Eve was frustrated that there was nothing she could do to spare the child from reliving the horrors that she'd seen and experienced. At least Caitlin would know that Lionel Coyle would never be able to hurt her or anyone else again.

"The cut on your head isn't new," Lisa said. "The airbag blowing up in your face opened up the old wound. You're lucky your injuries aren't a lot worse."

"I was just doing my job."

"The hell you were. Suicide isn't part of your job description. It's a miracle you're both alive. Don't get me wrong, I'm thankful for what you did, probably everybody in the country is going to be when they hear about it. But I could have lost you today because you acted without thinking."

Eve saw tears in her sister's eyes. "I was thinking of Caitlin."

"I'd appreciate it if you'd think of yourself now and then."

"In a way, I was. I couldn't live with myself if I was right about her being alive and she'd burned to death in that house."

Lisa was finished with the cast and peeled off her rubber gloves. "I'd get you a sling for your arm, but I know you won't use it or the Vicodin the doctor prescribed for pain. So my prescription is that you go home, eat a half gallon of Ben & Jerry's Chunky Monkey, and binge on the *Terminator* movies."

"I can do that."

Eve's phone vibrated beside her on the gurney. She picked it up with her left hand and saw a text from Duncan informing her that he was outside and on his way in.

"I've got to go," Eve said. She slid off the gurney and hugged her sister. "Thanks for patching me up."

"I'll come by later tonight with extra meds," Lisa said.

"Oreo cookies?"

"With double stuff."

"Isn't that extreme?" Eve said. "I have a broken wrist, I'm not dying of cancer."

Eve gave her sister a kiss on the cheek and headed out to the lobby, where two deputies were stationed. She emerged just as Duncan came in from the parking lot with Cleve Kenworth, who rushed up to Eve so fast, she was afraid he might tackle her.

"Is it true?" Cleve asked. "Is Caitlin really alive?"

"She's severely dehydrated and confused, but the doctors say she'll be fine. She's in exam room five. One of the deputies will take you back."

"I can't believe it." Cleve started to tear up. "I don't know how to thank you."

"Take her home, keep her safe, and give her that *Brady Bunch* family you told me about."

Cleve gave her a firm hug, took a deep breath, and went back into the ER with a deputy, leaving her with Duncan.

"It's an amazing thing you did today," he said.

"Not insane?"

"Oh, it was that, too. But I figure you've heard that enough already."

"Thanks," she said.

"The captain is furious, ranting about insubordination and the Explorer you destroyed, but I think he'll overlook it given the circumstances."

"And if I don't tell anybody that he and the sheriff didn't believe me that Caitlin was alive and being held captive."

"All that matters is that Caitlin's safe."

Duncan tipped his head toward the doors to the ER and lowered his voice to a near whisper. "Did Coyle sexually abuse her?"

Eve shrugged. She didn't know and she didn't want to think about it, not now anyway. "The house is ashes but I got pictures of the crime scene before we fled."

Duncan looked at her in disbelief. "You *did?*"

"Of course. Wouldn't you?"

"Hell no," Duncan said. "But I wouldn't have been there in the first place. I value my life. Running into a raging wildfire on a hunch is suicidal."

"It was more than a hunch. You heard me present the evidence to Moffett and Lansing. It was a certainty."

"Only to you," Duncan said. "I'm not ashamed

that I was unconvinced. You were right this time, but next time you might not be."

"Then next time you'll just have to come along to keep me out of trouble."

"Not me. I'll be working on my long putt in Palm Springs."

"You've still got one hundred and sixty-one days to go before that happens."

"One hundred sixty," he said.

"A lot could happen between now and then. Has the word gone out yet that Caitlin is alive?"

Duncan shook his head. "Lansing is still trying to figure out how to spin it."

"That's great." Eve took him by the arm and started hustling him toward the door. "You need to take me downtown to see Coyle."

"Now?"

"Lights and siren and pedal to the floor," she said. "I want Coyle to hear the news from me."

Lionel Coyle was waiting for Eve in the visitor's room in the Men's Central Jail. She left Duncan in the hallway and went in alone. Coyle broke into a big smile when he saw her.

"Ouch," he said. "What happened to you?"

She sat down across the table from him. "I had a car accident. I came here straight from the hospital."

"Of course you did. The clock is ticking and

the moment of truth is tomorrow morning. You didn't want to waste a second."

"No, I didn't."

"I knew you'd be back today. You want to know why?" He leaned forward, arms on the table, and looked her in the eye. "Because my lawyer *dismembered* you. Are you ready for our selfie?"

"I'll take it later, when you're strapped to a table, getting your lethal injection."

He laughed. "Is that the best you've got?"

She leaned forward now, not breaking eye contact. "I've got Caitlin."

Coyle tried to sustain his smile but it wavered at the edges. "You must have banged your head real hard in that accident. You're not making sense."

"She's alive. I found her under the floor of that empty house near Malibu Creek State Park. I wanted you to hear it from me first."

Coyle's smile vanished and his face went pale so fast that Eve thought he might be about to throw up. She sat back, just in case.

"I'll make a deal with you," he said.

"You don't have anything I want."

"I'll tell you where the bodies are."

"I know where they are, Lionel. They're in the ruins of the old *Planet of the Apes* set."

"But you don't know exactly where, do you? It's a big park. I can take you straight to them. On one condition." He leaned forward again and whispered, "After I show you where the bodies are, maybe on the way back to the car, you let me escape, and then shoot me dead before I get away."

It was an outrageous request and it surprised her. "Why would I want to do that?"

"Think of all the publicity," he said.

He wanted his death to be fast, and memorable, and it sickened her that he believed she'd actually go for it just so she could have a few more minutes of fame.

She stood up. "I'm going to enjoy watching you die."

"Wait!" he said.

But Eve turned her back on him and walked out of the room. Duncan was leaning against a wall, scrolling through something on his phone screen, when she stepped into the hallway.

"How did it go?" Duncan asked, looking up from his phone.

"He wanted to make a deal."

"A little late for that. The news broke while you were inside with him. Your video is going viral."

"I don't see why." Eve started walking down the hall, Duncan falling into step beside her. "The video is old news."

"Not that one. I'm talking about *Deathfist II*, your new viral video."

"I don't have a new video."

"Yes you do. There was a camera mounted

on the chopper that picked you up. One of the firefighters leaked the video to the press. It's you with Caitlin in your arms, running across a field, chased by a firestorm. It's pretty amazing stuff."

He stopped and showed her the video on his phone. The woman on-screen, her bloody face set in grim determination, held the child tight to her chest and ran toward the camera, the tongues of flame licking at her back. Eve didn't see herself in the video. It was as if the woman with the blood and soot on her face was somebody else.

Duncan pocketed his phone. "Don't let me forget to get your autograph once the cast is off."

Eve suddenly felt very tired. "You know what I really need right now?"

"A William Morris agent?"

"A donut," she said.

"That's the best idea you've had since the day we met." He smiled, put a fatherly arm around her, and gently led her toward the security gate. "I'm starting to think you might just make it as a homicide detective, though I suppose now you'll want to be sheriff."

"Not yet," Eve said.

"You sure? After what you did today, and this video, you could probably win the election in a landslide."

"I think I still have a few more things to learn."

"That's the first lesson right there," he said.

"The second is never get a donut filled with anything because it's going to end up on your shirt."

"You're a fount of wisdom, Duncan."

# AUTHOR'S NOTE AND ACKNOWLEDGMENTS

This novel is entirely a work of fiction but it was inspired by an actual case that I learned about as one of three civilian guests attending a professional homicide investigators training seminar in Green Bay, Wisconsin.

I couldn't have written this book without the patient help of Joe Dietz and Daniel Winterich, two of the law enforcement officers who conducted that investigation, presented the case at the seminar, and then allowed me to bombard them with questions for weeks afterward.

I'm also indebted to several other past and present law enforcement officers for their wise counsel—including Paul Bishop, Robin Burcell, David Putnam, and Lee Lofland.

And, finally, I'm grateful to authors Melinda Leigh and Kendra Elliot, the other two civilians at the seminar, for letting me take dibs on this great story.

The wildfire at the end of this book is also a work of fiction . . . or at least it was when I wrote it.

I completed this novel months before the Woolsey Fire swept through Thousand Oaks, Oak Park, Agoura, Bell Canyon, West Hills,

Calabasas, and Malibu in November 2018, eventually burning 97,000 acres and 1,600 structures during its devastating march to the sea.

The fire forced me and my family to evacuate our Calabasas home and seek shelter with my sister in Santa Clarita. One of the things I brought with me (among the important papers, jewelry, family photos, artwork, et cetera that we hurriedly gathered and stuffed in the car) was the copyedited manuscript for this book, which my editor had sent me a few days earlier to proofread.

So I found myself in the surreal situation of editing my scenes of a wildfire sweeping through Malibu Creek State Park as the same events I had imagined were happening live on TV.

I'm glad to say our home survived the fire, though the flames came frighteningly close . . . almost as close as my fiction came to reality.

# ABOUT THE AUTHOR

Lee Goldberg is a two-time Edgar Award and two-time Shamus Award nominee and the #1 *New York Times* bestselling author of more than thirty novels, including the Ian Ludlow thrillers *Killer Thriller* and *True Fiction*, *King City*, *The Walk*, fifteen Monk mysteries, and the internationally bestselling Fox & O'Hare books (*The Heist*, *The Chase*, *The Job*, *The Scam*, and *The Pursuit*) cowritten with Janet Evanovich. He has also written and/or produced many TV shows, including *Diagnosis Murder*, *SeaQuest*, and *Monk*, and is the co-creator of the Hallmark movie series *Mystery 101*. As an international television consultant, he has advised networks and studios in Canada, France, Germany, Spain, China, Sweden, and the Netherlands on the creation, writing, and production of episodic television series. You can find more information about Lee and his work at www.leegoldberg.com.

## Center Point Large Print
600 Brooks Road / PO Box 1
Thorndike, ME 04986-0001 USA

**(207) 568-3717**

**US & Canada:**
**1 800 929-9108**
www.centerpointlargeprint.com

*Dear readers, if you wish to initial/ mark that you've read this book please make your mark here.*

| | | | | |
|---|---|---|---|---|
| | | | | |
| | | | | |
| | | | | |